White as Witching

This is a work of fiction. All of the characters, organizations, and events are either products of the author's imagination or are used fictitiously.

WHITE AS WITCHING. Copyright © 2022 by Katherine Buel. All rights reserved.

Previously published as Heart of Snow

No part of this publication may be reproduced, distributed, or transmitted in any form or by any means, including photocopying, recording, or other electronic or mechanical methods, without the prior written permission of the publisher, except in the case of brief quotations for review purposes.

ISBN-13: 979-8845843753

Books by Katherine Buel

THE NORSE SAGA OF SIGURD
A Stranger at the Hearth
The Roots of Yggdrasil

THE GRIEVER'S MARK
The Griever's Mark
Chains of Water and Stone
Unbound

White as Witching

White *as* Witching

KATHERINE BUEL

Part 1.

The Wicked Queen

1.

A Rule, Broken

Every witch knows that words have power.

Every queen knows that not all power is magic.

That was why my aunt Lyric, Witch-Queen of Cresilea, called her yearly tithe the Selection. Selection implied chosen. Selection implied opportunity. If folk noticed that the five girls selected each year were never heard from again? Well, what could you expect when they'd left their simple village lives behind for the glamour of life at court?

I knew better than to believe such tales because I knew my aunt. She had murdered my family, after all.

But that wasn't the beginning.

So what was the beginning?

I might say, *Once upon a time, a queen gave birth to two daughters, one as rosy and fair as the dawn and the other with skin as white as snow and hair as dark as ebony.*

Or I might say, *Once upon a time, a queen with two daughters died, and their father the king wed their aunt, who killed him and took his throne.*

Or perhaps, *Once upon a time, a man walked into a village holding the hand of a girl with skin as white as snow and hair as dark as ebony, a child who might have been beautiful—if not for her ruined face.*

After seven years in the remote village of Thistledown, my first eleven in the royal castle felt like a dream of another life. My fingers had long forgotten the sleek glide of silk ribbons and the cool delicacy of silver spoons. Here, I was only Gala, the blacksmith's daughter with the scar that disfigured the left side of her face.

A shame, the folk of Thistledown still sometimes said, that I had fallen into the forge as a child, but such things did happen. They were glad, at least, that it had happened before Halen and I had come to Thistledown. "You've left your bad luck behind," they often said in those early days, pleased to have a blacksmith and willing to accept his burned daughter into the bargain.

We didn't look much alike, Halen and I, but no one could really see past my scar. That was the point of it. That was why Halen had burned me—to hide me in ugliness.

In those days, with the name Snow White fresh upon everyone's lips, a pretty girl with pale skin and dark hair, who happened to be eleven years old, could not have been easily hidden. Everyone was looking for her and the other princess. They would not find Rose, but they might find me.

The story was that King Philip had been assassinated by a neighboring king—and what a story to spread like wildfire through Cresilea. Oh, but imagine the tragedy of such a wedding night! The king, murdered right there in the Great Hall! And in the middle of his first dance with his new bride!

I didn't need to imagine. I had been there, so I knew full well that Lyric had driven the blade in herself.

The story told, however, made Lyric the widow, the victim, the bereaved. And to have lost her two nieces the same night? Such devastation! Both princesses had been stolen away, you see—according to the tale.

Odd, some might think, that when Lyric's forces took revenge on her neighbor, the supposed assassin, killing that king and adding his lands to her own, neither hide nor hair of either princess had been seen. No doubt the girls had been foully murdered and their bodies disposed of. "Terrible," folk said for years, shaking their heads with that mixture of horror and relish reserved for tragedy that has befallen someone else.

There was no relish for me. Never will I forget Rose's scream as one of Lyric's silver-clad servants grabbed her in the midst of the chaos.

My luck ran stronger that night. It was Halen, longtime captain of the guard and friend of my father's, who grabbed me. Seven years later, I could recall only flashes of our flight through the castle and the moonlit gardens to the secret gate. With the castle crowning a steep, scrubby tor, our path down must have been barely fit for the nimble hooves of goats, but I had no memory of that part. Maybe Halen did, but who could know? The only person who shared the secret was me, and we had never spoken of that night.

Not once in seven years.

It was June, the tail end of morel season.

In Thistledown, those honeycombed mushrooms were met with more *oohs!* and *ahhs!* than greeted emeralds in the royal court. Since I was the only one who would forage for them, I could price them high.

Risking spiders and slugs and leaf mold, I crawled through the low, secret places that morels like to grow. The damp of the forest floor seeped through my blue homespun at the knees and elbows as I used my small knife to snip the hollow stems. I was stuffing a handful into my burlap sack when I heard it.

It's strange how the sound of a child laughing can chill you. In the wrong place, at the wrong time, nothing is eerier.

The reason I was the only one who went morel hunting was that I was the only one who would enter the woods. Children in particular were forbidden to set foot in them. It was easy to get lost with no horizon and all the trees looking the same. It was easy to get hurt from slipping on a mossy rock or stepping in an unseen hole. But it was the Fae that folk truly feared.

The woods bordering Thistledown—and all the other villages and towns between here and the royal city of Orlas—

served as a buffer between our human lands and the Brightwood, where the Fae dwelled. The High Fae, who looked more or less human, rarely ventured beyond the Brightwood's borders, but the little faeries and other strange creatures haunted the buffering woods. They loved to toy with humans, tempting them down faerie paths with music and bright flowers and berries that gleamed like jewels.

Such had always been their way, but in the years since Lyric had taken Cresilea, the creatures of the woods had grown exceptionally wild and strange. I heard them on occasion. Little tittering voices. An odd sequence of high musical notes. Once I had even caught a flash of tiny blue wings from the corner of my eye.

I knew to ignore them. Even as a sheltered princess I had been taught caution. But a child with a burned face learns to be alone, and often such a child ventures into places that others do not. Halen had given up scolding me years ago and now would only grumble, "Be careful."

So when I heard a child laughing out there in the woods I knew something was very, very wrong.

I rocked up to a kneeling position, sitting back on my boot heels to listen. Hearing nothing, I dared to hope I had imagined it. My mind played such tricks sometimes, tormenting me with a glimpse of red hair that vanished or a ghostly word that made me spin and look for Rose. *She is dead*, I would remind myself harshly.

Realizing I'd dropped my knife, I picked it up and went back to work—until, high and delighted and unmistakably human, the laughter drifted to me through the trees once more. Now that, I had not imagined.

Swinging my foraging sack around to my back, I started off through the woodland patchwork of golden light and umber shadows. My fingers clenched around my harvesting knife, but its small presence offered little reassurance.

Branches and brambles caught at my skirt and snagged my long ebony hair from its braid, but I paid them no mind. I had to focus on my path, had to remember it.

It occurred to me that this might be a trick, the sound a mimicry of human laughter, a trap for a fool like myself, but there are some things you must do, even when they are foolish. I paused by the stream. It was a landmark I knew, something I could follow home. The stream wound through the woods like a snake, and a coil of its watery body curved out of the woods near our cottage to feed the forge. The stream also marked my personal boundary. I had never ventured beyond it.

That sound of childish joy pealed through the woods again, closer now, and I splashed through the stream, soaking my boots, and hurried up a short rise.

A path of wild purple iris, white lilies, and yellow rue wended through the trees. Normally, I would wrench my eyes away from such a sight, but I followed it desperately now. And there she was: the baker's thirteen-year-old daughter, clad in a yellow dress, clapping her hands with delight as a ring of tiny faeries with butterfly wings lowered a wreath of flowers onto her head, settling the crown among her blonde curls.

"Margret!"

She spun, her round cheeks flushed with pleasure. "Oh, Gala, look! Isn't it beautiful?"

"Quite so. Come with me." I held out my hand.

"I don't want to." She turned to look down the faerie path. It stretched into the distance and out of sight.

The faeries buzzed around her, a flurry of colorful wings. They snatched up tendrils of her blonde hair and tugged. One perched on her shoulder. It raised a tiny flute to its lips and played a light strain of music into her ear. Margret swayed in time.

I crept closer, my heart pounding, my boots crushing the delicate flowers. Some of the faeries left Margret to buzz around me as I took her hand. Her eyes lifted to mine with a hazy, enchanted glaze upon them. My father's eyes had looked like that in the days between my mother's death and his second wedding, when Lyric had bewitched him.

"Ow!" Margret exclaimed when my hand tightened involuntarily on hers.

I gave her arm a shake. "Stop this nonsense. We're going back."

"I don't want to," she repeated. "I burned the bread. Mother yelled at me."

A faerie grabbed a lock of my hair and gave it a sharp tug. I released Margret's hand to swat at the little creature. It darted away, chittering angrily.

Margret made a platform of her hands. A faerie alighted on her upturned palms and danced, shivering its dazzling purple wings, its tiny body shimmering with the leaves it wore as clothes. Strings of white seeds looped out from twig-thin limbs. I pinned my eyes to the ground—and saw roots slithering up through the faerie path.

"Margret—"

"Mother said she wished she had given birth to a goat instead of me because at least a goat would be useful."

"It's your mother who's a goat—an old goat. Don't you think?"

Margret's gasp of shock made her hands jerk. The dancing faerie fluttered upward with a chirp of indignation. As Margret clapped her hands to her mouth to stifle a nervous giggle, some of the haze cleared from her eyes. "Oh, Gala! She might put you in the oven for that!"

"She could try. Maybe I'd put *her* in the oven."

Margret's big brown eyes turned sad. "I wish I was like you. You don't care what people say."

"You don't need to care what people say when they say stupid things." As Margret chewed at her bottom lip, eyes clearing further, the faeries began to buzz around us like bees shaken from a hive. I pressed, "Let's go home."

This time when I held out my hand, Margret took it, but as she tried to step clear of the faerie path, the roots lashed around her ankles. My harvesting knife had never left my hand, and I slashed at the roots with its small blade. They hissed like snakes and snapped at my hands. Margret tried to tear away but fell to her rear on the faerie path. The flowers bobbed with mocking gentleness, and the roots began to twine around her wrists.

It was her scream that broke the lock inside me. It took me back, instantly, to that final night in the Great Hall, to the last sound I ever heard from my sister. That awful, fateful scream. Without even thinking, I broke Halen's one and only rule: *do not use magic.*

Seven years I had obeyed that rule.

Seven years I had kept my magic locked inside me, not touching it, not tempting it, not allowing myself to even think about it.

It wasn't just fear of exposing my identity that made Halen forbid its use. In a place like Thistledown, a witch made for a convenient scapegoat for any misfortune: a sick child, a poor harvest, a storm that damaged someone's roof. But when Margret's scream hit my ears, magic came roaring out of me. Words tumbled free.

"Back into the earth, you wretched roots! Wither, flowers; scatter, wings! Be *gone*!"

Hissing and shrieking, the roots released Margret's limbs and retracted. The flowers shrank and shriveled, and the faeries went buzzing off, dashing through light and shadow until they vanished from sight.

Margret pulled her arms in, crossing them over her heart. Her knees were drawn up. Her crown of flowers had shriveled into fragile threads. Tears streamed down her cheeks, and her eyes were wide with terror. But of the faeries and roots? Or of me?

What I had done crashed down upon me, and I returned my knife to its sheath with a shaking hand. I unknotted my kerchief from my neck and held it out to Margret. Her eyes met mine at last then she flung herself at me. For a second, I thought she was attacking me, but her arms tightened around my waist and she sobbed against my breast. The remains of her crown turned to ash and drifted away.

"Erm …" I patted her back awkwardly.

I had never been good at this sort of thing. "Such a cold fish!" I recalled hearing one of the court ladies whisper when I didn't melt sufficiently at her compliment.

"Time to go back," I announced, tugging Margret to her feet. When she sniffled, I handed her the kerchief. She took it and blew her nose.

Every sign of the faerie path was gone, but I tracked carefully back the way I'd come, Margret practically treading on my heels, and found the stream. Thank the gods. I had half expected it to be gone like the path of flowers, another trick of the faeries.

I busied myself seeking my other landmarks. I didn't want to think about what I'd done, the rule I'd broken, the fact that Margret had seen. Or the fact that it had felt, for a moment, like freedom.

"Gala?"

My heart skipped. She was going to ask about my magic. "Yes?"

"Will you ... please not tell my mother?"

I sagged with relief. "Why would I tell that old goat a thing?"

A hint of sparkle returned to Margret's eyes. "You really think she's an old goat?"

I clambered up a rocky incline and helped Margret to the top. "She's worse than Prickle."

Margret let out a squeak of laughter. My goat Prickle had a reputation in Thistledown. She was a biter, a kicker, and every time she escaped, which was often, she ate someone's laundry off the line or found her way onto someone's roof and screamed her head off about it.

I brushed at my skirts. "But don't tell her I said that. Your mother is terrifying."

"Not to you. You're not scared of anything."

Brave Snowdrop. That was what my mother used to call me, and Gala was its echo. Galanthus. The snowdrop. A lie—I was terrified all the time. But I kept my fear locked away like my magic, as though it didn't exist. There is plenty of space inside a person to hide things.

"Oh, no!" Margret exclaimed.

I spun, heart leaping into my throat. "What—"

"I dropped your kerchief!"

"Oh." I clutched at my chest, willing my heart to settle. Brave Snowdrop indeed.

"I'm such a dimwit," Margret said miserably.

"Don't talk like that."

"I'm sorry," she insisted.

"It's just a stupid kerchief. It's nothing."

But it was something to me. Red flowers against a blue background—my father's colors. Still. It *was* just a kerchief. I certainly wasn't going back for it.

We reached the edge of the wood, where Gil Hensen's hayfield stretched between the last trees and the village. The grass rippled peacefully green under the sun.

"We should separate," I said. "I don't want you to get in trouble." I had my morels to sell; everyone would know where I'd been. If Margret and I returned together, they would know where she had been as well.

"I won't tell anyone," Margret said, hugging her arms around herself. "About … you know. I understand."

"Yes, well …" I trailed off, unsure what to say. The damage was done.

Margret chewed at her lip, hesitating. Then she flung her arms around me once more, driving the air out of me. "Thank you, Gala," she whispered fiercely before taking off at a run through the hayfield.

I walked along the edge of the woods so I could enter Thistledown from a different direction than Margret. My foraging sack lacked the heft I might have hoped for, but I wasn't going back for more. I wouldn't be returning to the woods for a good long while.

Or so I told myself.

My day went from bad to worse as I reached the Thistledown Inn, where I hoped to sell the morels to Annette, the Inn's owner. I was climbing the porch steps when Corbin spoke behind me.

"And where has our little curiosity been today?"

It wasn't until his sneering tone hit my ears that I realized how the incident in the woods had affected me. Not the incident—Margret. Her awkward hug, her ... awe of me. So different from the terrible, shuddering awe of someone taking in the sight of my face.

You're not scared of anything.

Thank you, Gala.

I had not recognized the subtle thawing inside myself until Corbin's voice made me stiffen, until I felt it all freeze over again.

Feet planted on the porch steps, I twisted to face him and replied, "My curiosity led me straight to a valuable patch of morels. A good day, I'd call it."

I knew what he'd meant, of course, that *I* was "our little curiosity," but I also knew it would gall him if I seemed to miss his point.

A muscle ticked in Corbin's jaw. His eyes drifted, as usual, to the patch of wrinkled, shiny scarring that marred the left

14

side of my face from cheekbone to jaw and tugged down the corner of my mouth. He always looked at me like that, like he couldn't believe his eyes even after all these years.

What did I care? Beauty had never done a thing for me, but ugliness had saved my life.

Corbin shook his head, rueful but somehow relishing. "Maybe you'll be worth it, if he gets the forge."

He meant Sam, Halen's apprentice. Though we weren't betrothed, many expected it. Sam could inherit the forge through me and become Thistledown's blacksmith after Halen. While Sam might marry a girl of better looks, none could set him up with a ready forge.

I shrugged, indifferent to it all.

"High and mighty, for a little hag," Corbin seethed.

And yet, there was always something hungry in his gaze when he looked at me. He'd asked Halen for my hand last year. By Thistledown standards, Corbin was a man of average looks and average prosperity. No particular desperation would have driven him to choose me. He had actually wanted me. It would have given him pleasure, I suppose, to stare at me all the time, to constantly express his disgust. It frustrated him that I didn't care.

Indifference is a form of power.

I stared at Corbin, icy and untouched, until he muttered something and wandered off down Thistledown's main road. I stared him all the way to the chandler's house before I continued up the steps to the Inn.

With few travelers to accommodate, the Inn mostly served cider and beer and potpies, plus the occasional delicacy, to our local folk, making the Inn's common room the place to get news when there was any or gossip when there wasn't.

This early in the day, the place was empty, the massive hearth lying cold, no one sitting in the worn armchairs or spilling beer on the tables.

Behind the bar, Annette was wrangling a heavy keg across the floor. Widowed, she had no man to take over such tasks, and she made clear often enough that she wanted none. I liked Annette.

"Tell me that fool left," she grunted then gave up on the keg, straightening. She flicked her graying brown braid over her shoulder.

"Long gone."

The fact that Annette had observed my interaction with Corbin but not interfered was another reason I liked her. She understood that I did not want to be rescued.

She nodded to the keg. "Help me with this thing."

I slung my foraging sack onto the bar and went to join Annette. Each grabbing a side, we hefted the keg into place. My muscles screamed at the weight, and I let out a satisfying grunt of exertion.

Annette swiped a sleeve across her brow and reached for one of the hanging pewter tankards. The tankards formed a disjointed, cloudy mirror, blurring my face until it looked no more remarkable than Annette's.

She held the tankard under the keg's tap and released a stream of golden cider. She plunked it onto the bar and declared, "Helper's fee."

I tasted the cider. "Sweet," I pronounced.

"Too sweet?"

"I prefer more bite, but I think others will like it."

Annette whipped a cloth from her belt and polished a spot on the bar. "Let's hope. I could barely give away that red ale."

"That's because it tasted like—"

"I know, I know." She waved me off then eyed my foraging sack critically. "Looks light."

Usually, I could hold my own against Annette's fierce haggling, but I was a shade too eager to be rid of that reminder of the woods. The agitated, impatient feeling I'd been struggling to squash down since breaking Halen's rule didn't help.

I had *used magic*.

After seven years of keeping it locked inside I'd let it burst out—but only for the briefest moment. I'd shoved it back down, and it seemed to pace within me like a caged animal.

By the time I'd settled with Annette and was walking home with one of her older laying hens squawking in my foraging sack, my whole body was shaking.

Would this be my life, my whole life, living this way, stifled and hiding? Bearing only a shadow of my name—being only a shadow of myself?

Better, I thought, to face my murderous aunt.

In a different season, Halen might have noticed my lack of appetite. In summer, he was always too tired to notice anything but the mountain of work to be done: horses to shoe, plows to sharpen, wheels to repair.

Seven years of hard work had aged Halen well beyond his fifty summers, grizzling his once sandy hair and leaving his face lined and careworn. He'd developed the country habit of eating with rolled up sleeves, exposing the bulging forearms and meaty, toughened hands that spoke of his hours at the forge.

I wondered sometimes if he mourned the loss of his old life, if he regretted helping me escape. He never said so, but he wasn't happy here. He never smiled. I remembered him smiling, long ago, at something my father had said.

The two of us ate at the rustic table that marked the boundary between the kitchen and sitting room. A fire crackled in the fieldstone hearth, expanding on the light of our glass-faced lantern, making the shadows flicker and dance across the table and our faces.

"She'll be making her selection soon." Halen dropped it out of nowhere, but even so I knew who *she* was.

I chased my uneaten roast around my plate with my fork. "They've never come here."

Thistledown lay at the edge of Cresilea with little beyond it but woods and mountains. Plenty of towns and villages offered a multitude of girls that might be more easily *selected*.

"Still." He got up from the table and walked his plate over to the copper sink.

Still, what? I wanted to reply, even though I knew what he was saying, that he would not allow them to take me.

We had this conversation every year, and every year it angered me. Because what it really meant was: we are in hiding and always will be. Nothing will ever change. It meant I would never use my magic again. It meant I was supposed to marry Sam and start a family and eat roast beef at this table for the rest of my life and never speak of my murdered parents, my murdered sister, or my wicked aunt.

But I could not picture that future. I had never been able to.

There was an awful truth I rarely acknowledged: sometimes I almost hated Halen for saving me. Sometimes, I wanted to demand, *What was the point?*

I never demanded that because we never spoke of the past. Maybe that was why I could not imagine a future here. How can a future grow out of nothing?

It cannot. The past, along with our decisions, makes the future. That was one of the few things that, later, Lyric and I would agree on.

It is the essence of revenge, after all.

2.

Silver Cloaks and Poison

A week later, my magic was slumbering again like a hibernating bear, and I performed all the duties that shaped my life in Thistledown. I cooked and cleaned while Halen and Sam worked the forge. I tended our animals and garden. I traded goods in town and sometimes delivered Halen's finished work to customers. On the day I saw the queen's silver, I was out gathering herbs in the high meadows above Thistledown.

Hours of ranging across the fields had filled my burlap sack with an array of herbs for the teas, salves, and tinctures that I made. My mother had been a keen gardener. I recalled some of her lessons, and one of my treasures was a book of herb lore I'd stolen from a peddler's cart while he was drunk at the Inn. When Halen asked where I'd gotten the book, for books were rare in Thistledown, I claimed the peddler had given it to me out of pity. When your whole life is a lie, you think nothing of minor deceptions.

And maybe ... I had hoped to see Halen to flinch at my reminder of what he'd done. Maybe I had wanted him to say, just once, *I'm sorry.*

But he had only looked away.

Prickle noticed the queen's company before I did. I had brought her and her two kids with me so I could keep an eye on the fiend. As Prickle's gaze locked somewhere, her tail flicked with agitation.

"What?" I asked her, pushing away the kids, who thought my being crouched in the grass meant I was offering myself as something to jump on. "Did a leaf move and scare you? Is there a dangerous squirrel on the loose?" In addition to being mean, Prickle was highly dramatic.

As both kids darted to Prickle's side, I rubbed my arm where one of their sharp hooves had scraped me. "Good riddance," I muttered.

Then I followed Prickle's gaze.

Where the dirt road into Thistledown brushed the woods, a carriage of shimmering silver and glossy black had appeared. Two black horses pulled it, and a driver cloaked in the queen's silver occupied the high bench. Astride more black horses, three silver-cloaked riders traveled behind it. Ahead of them all, another black horse bore a figure in green. I should have seen such a flashy company from a mile away, but here it was, nearly upon Thistledown.

Despite the June sun that had me sweating, I shivered, and my chest went so tight I couldn't breathe. I had not seen Lyric's silver in seven years, and a panicked voice inside me cried, *Hide!*

Then something colder and harder silenced that voice, stilling me utterly as I watched that gleaming company make its way toward Thistledown with only one possible purpose.

The Selection.

Thistledown was a flurry of activity by the time I arrived with Prickle and the kids. Six different people told me the news before I reached the Inn. Everyone started with words like "her majesty" and "opportunity" and "girls" and "our." Then they would stutter out words like "erm" or "well" and get red-faced before hailing someone else and hurrying away.

A burned girl, they knew, would never be chosen.

Through the windows of the Inn, I spotted silver cloaks amid the crowd of local folk. Even if I had wanted to go in for a closer look, I couldn't leave Prickle and the kids unattended. There was no telling what they might destroy if Prickle slipped her collar.

"Oi!" I shouted as she attempted just that. I hooked my foot around her hindquarters to stop her. She tried to bite me.

I headed on down the road, practically dragging her. I needed to get her and the kids home. They were clinging to her sides now, but the one with the black ear sometimes bolted.

Sam came out from the forge when I arrived. I ignored him to return Prickle and the kids to their paddock, latching the gate and tying the ropes that would hold it shut after

Prickle nosed the latch. Instead of going away as I'd hoped, Sam waited for me.

His wide-eyed, slightly dazed look—as well as Halen's furious hammering ringing out from the forge—told me that the news had reached them ahead of me.

"I was in town," he said vaguely, one hand flapping in the general direction of the road.

He'd hustled his way here, it seemed, to bring Halen the news. I grimaced at the thought of the argument waiting for me in the forge. I had hoped to choose my moment and deliver the news myself, in my own way.

I said, "You should go home, Sam." He had a sister of sixteen. Ruth would stand with me and the other girls tomorrow on the village green. "Your family has a lot to discuss."

Not that discussion would mean anything. The queen's representatives would make their choice and no one could change that. A few coins would drop into the hands of the selected girl's family. Her bride price, they called it.

As one of Thistledown's prettiest girls, Ruth would seem to stand a chance. I wondered at Sam's hurrying here instead of home. He had never sneered at me as Corbin and some of the others did, but that was a mark of his decency, not of affection. It surprised me, then, when his hand caught mine. His fingers were rough with calluses; they were strong. And foreign. He had never touched me before. Corbin's words rose up: *Maybe you'll be worth it, if he gets the forge.*

I pulled away.

"It's a chance," he said, as everyone did about the Selection. His eyes darted to mine as though to gauge my reaction, as though to see whether I wanted that chance for myself. I stiffened, both at the delusion about Lyric's motives and at his attempt to know my feelings. They were none of his business.

I stared at him until he looked away. It annoyed me that he pretended I *had* a chance in a beauty contest. It annoyed me that he pretended my face didn't matter. I had seen him speak with other girls—casually, comfortably, with a smile. He was only ever awkward with me. He was trying, I supposed, for Halen's sake. Or because I would be worth it, if he got the forge? Whatever the case, I wished he would stop.

Besides, I had bigger things to think about. After Sam finally left, I eyed the forge. Halen's hammering had never ceased.

"She will not take you," he announced the instant I stepped inside.

No fear showed in his eyes, and no warmth either. It had never been love that had bound him to me, but honor and duty. I saw it so clearly as the blacksmith vanished, like an enchantment that had been laid over him for seven years. All at once, he was a soldier again, never mind that he stood sweating at the anvil in his leather apron with the forge fire glowing behind him and the tools of his unwanted trade hung all about.

"They will not choose me," I told him. He had made sure that beauty would never betray me.

"They cannot choose you if you're not there."

"They won't choose a girl with half a face."

Did my words bring the memory back to him as they brought it back to me? How he had lifted the red-hot pan from the campfire. How he had said, *Close your eyes, Snow.*

Don't look. It had taken me a year to tolerate the smell of cooking meat.

My words seemed to shrink and shrivel him as my magic had shrunk and shriveled the faerie path. He caved in on himself like a wizened old man, frail and spent. It lasted but a moment. He straightened, casting off my words.

"Don't act the fool," he said. "Whatever Lyric wants with the girls, it's not to marry them off." Maybe the girls were chosen for their demureness or the color of their hair or the sound of their voices. Maybe they were chosen for sport.

I argued, "Attendance at the Selection is mandatory. My absence would draw more attention than my presence. Questions might be asked. Why risk that?" *And why do you care?* That was what I really wanted to know.

"You are the rightful queen, Snow."

"What does that matter—here in Thistledown?" It angered me, that name suddenly on his lips after seven years, the past we had never spoken of.

"It matters."

"And yet you would have me marry Sam and live here as though I am not."

"I would have you *live.*"

"To what purpose, if I am here?"

"It's my duty, Snow."

It was then, as his words crushed me with the very truth I had already known, that I realized I'd been harboring some small and foolish hope that he would say, *Because I love you. Because I could not bear for anything to happen to you.* But it was my bloodline that mattered to him, and for no reason except that, former captain that he was, he did not know what else to value—even here, where it was valueless.

It was for the best. The fact that he did not love me made it easier for me to lie to him.

"There is no reason to throw away our life here," I argued. "If we flee, we might be pursued. At the very least, it would raise questions. Better to hide in plain sight. It has worked until now. It will work for one more day."

"It might. It might not."

"Lyric is not here. No one who knows me is here. But you would make us conspicuous. You would pull her gaze this way."

Halen frowned. There was some truth in my words, and he could not ignore it. "I need to think, Gala. We'll discuss this after dinner."

As much as it had angered me to hear the name Snow, at least I had felt something. As the name Gala was laid over me again, I froze inside.

That night, after I had poisoned Halen and he slumped at the table beside his soup, as the fire crackled in the hearth and the pieces of our life lay around us—my book of herb lore and the quilt I would never finish, the wooden horse he was carving in idle moments—I did not allow myself to feel regret. Halen would not die, but he would be too ill to rise until it was too late to stop me.

The village green had held parties of every kind for generations. It had never held a Selection before, and there was something awful about the sight of a dozen girls between the ages of thirteen and twenty lined up like livestock at market under Thistledown's old oak tree, where a scrap of pink and white checkered cloth, a streamer left over from Gil and Harley's wedding last fall, hung listlessly in the branches.

And yet, the girls wore their best dresses and had threaded ribbons and flowers through their hair, just as they did at any gathering on the green. No music drifted through the open air and none of the usual carefree laughter, but some of the girls whispered excitedly to each other, and a murmur of voices bubbled from the crowd that hovered at the edge of the green. Halen was not among them, of course.

The cloaked figures formed a cluster between our line and the crowd, like a piece of silver jewelry that had no place in our little world, but it was the man in the forest green tunic who drew all our eyes.

Man? He was no man. He was Fae—and not just any Fae but the queen's Fae. The Hunter.

While most of his kind did not venture from the Brightwood, the Hunter served Lyric. Like a wraith, he came and went, obeying her commands. What wickedness lay in his heart that he had abandoned his own kind to bind himself to the Witch-Queen of Cresilea?

It was wrong for him to be so beautiful, so unearthly in his perfection. The light seemed to delight in his fine cheekbones, to angle along his jaw almost worshipfully. Tall and lean, he moved along the line of girls with inhuman grace.

To my right, Sam's sister Ruth shifted uncertainly. How could she not? How could anyone not? The girls' country beauty, so mundane and human, was nothing in the face of that. For a moment, I was glad I had learned to live without it. As the Hunter made his graceful way down the line, the girls began looking around at each other with new eyes, as though to see what the Hunter might see, as though to say, *Who could possibly be fair enough?*

When Ruth's eyes flicked to me, her breath caught in surprise. Rarely did anyone see only my unblemished profile. Rarely did I let them. In a line, I had no choice. To my left, Myra saw only my ruin. But Ruth? With the scarring out of sight like the moon's dark side, the right half of my face told the story of a different girl, the beautiful one who might have been, the one who would have been *selected*. It is a strange thing to know how very beautiful you are by knowing how very ugly you are too.

"Sam always said you were pretty," Ruth breathed.

It jarred me. "He ... what?"

"But he knows you don't like him."

I frowned, feeling the tug against the immobile scarring of my left side. Even if others would let me forget how I looked, I could not. I could feel it in every hindered expression.

I said, "That's not true."

At least, I didn't think it was. I had never really considered it. Sam was simply ... there. He was part of a life I didn't want—one I was leaving.

"He's afraid of you, that's all." Ruth's eyes jumped to mine then away. "I'm telling you in case ... Well, *in case.*" In case she was selected, she meant. "You stare at people, you know. It makes them nervous."

These revelations jumbled about inside me. I did stare at people sometimes, challenging them with my ugliness, to show them I would not look away, would not look down, would not be made small by them. They had tried when I was young, the other girls in the village, many of whom stood in this line with me. Boys, too, who now stood in the crowd, watching. Even Ruth had once called me Wither Face.

That was all years ago because I had learned to not cry, to not look away. It gave them power. I would not apologize for defying them, for wrenching that power back from them.

But none of this mattered, not anymore, so I said, "I want nothing to do with cowards."

Yes, I meant her. Yes, I meant Sam. I meant everyone. I don't know if I *really* meant it, in my heart, but it freed something in me to say it. Words, after all, have power.

As Ruth edged away from me, bumping into Tillie on her other side, I returned my attention to the Hunter. Seeing that he had stopped in front of Margret sent a spike of fear through me. I had let Ruth distract me, and now the Hunter was eyeing Margret with far too much interest.

No!

Power cracked inside me like ice breaking on a river in spring. The Hunter staggered as though physically struck by the force of it. When his head whipped toward me and his eyes locked onto mine, I recoiled. I had meant to tempt him to me, to whisper at him, to make his eyes obsess over my ruined beauty as Corbin's did, to make myself the only thing he could see. I had hoped he would not even notice my magic.

But I had slapped him with it.

A man would have stridden toward me, body hulking my way, boots stomping out his authority. The Hunter, though, moved like light, or shadow perhaps. Something intangible that traveled in silence, barely noticed. Yet, when he stood before me, he was very, very real.

His beauty was both captivating and difficult to look at, overwhelming—and utterly inhuman. His hair tumbled to his shoulders in waves of rich brown such as I had seen only in the shadowed woods, and the tips of his pointed ears peeked through it. Then there was the unearthly luster of his skin—and those eyes. With their gentle hazel, they should have been beautiful. They would have been, with the least feeling in them. But they were horribly empty, as though he felt nothing in doing this wicked thing. I could not suppress my shudder.

But shudders pass.

I forced myself to straighten, to stand like iron before him. I stared at him as I had stared at so many others—in defiance, refusing to look away. He stared back.

A war started in his face. So still had his features been, so expressionless, that the sudden struggle shocked me. His lips flinched back in a snarl, exposing sharp incisors. His brow furrowed. Then he ripped his gaze away. His eyes, no longer so empty, arrowed to Margret.

No.

Those hazel eyes swung back to me, pupils contracting to eerie pinpricks. As the cords of his neck strung tight, I held his stare.

Choose.

Then he shuddered, as I had done, as though I were as terrible as he—and stepped back.

Horror crashed through me. I was losing him. I had *lost*.

No—he had. This was his surrender, for one silvery figure split off from the cluster. The woman moved toward us, toward me, across the village green. She had a stiff, slightly awkward gait, though maybe it only seemed that way after watching the Hunter. Her eyes were brown, her hair mousy-plain, her features unremarkable. As she stepped past the Hunter, he withdrew. She smiled at me as though in congratulations, but the smile was wooden.

"Whom do I pay?" Silver coins glinted between her thumb and forefinger.

"No one. I belong to myself."

She lifted an eyebrow then held the coins out to me, lightly clearing her throat at my hesitation. My hand came up jerkily, and the silver tumbled, cold and hard, onto my palm.

3.

Swallowed by Stone

As the carriage rolled from the sunlit road into the shadowy woods, I understood why I hadn't seen it from a mile off the day before. Though the route was more direct, it seemed impossible that such an elaborate conveyance could traverse the rugged woodland. On the opposite bench of black velvet, the woman who had handed me the silver coins sat, unconcerned, in her black dress. Her cloak lay on the seat beside her like a pool of molten silver.

"You may call me Fresia," she announced. "I will remain in attendance upon you on the way and in Orlas."

Though my years in Thistledown had constrained me in many ways, there had been freedoms. Solitude. Independence. The liberty to come and go without notice or explanation. So normal had that become for me that I'd forgotten the burden of attendance that was life at court—shadowed by others, rarely alone.

To hide my dismay, I said, "My name is Gala."

Fresia made no reply, as though she already knew my name, or didn't care.

I gazed out the window. The carriage rolled smoothly along when it should have been lurching over rocks and roots, tossing us about inside, creaking and groaning. It could only be magic. And what of the wilder magic here, the faeries and other creatures of the woods? With the Hunter as our guide, would they leave us alone? I saw no sign of wings or flower trails, heard no voices or strains of music.

One of the outriders appeared beyond the window. His face was unremarkable, but there was a greedy, hungering look in his eyes that had me pressing back into the velvet cushions. Fresia let out a little hiss, and the rider dropped back.

The hiss startled me, so feral sounding, but when my eyes jumped to Fresia I found only a bland expression on her face. Then she smiled as though in afterthought, as though to put me at ease. It did no such thing, not when the expression was as stiff now as it had been on the village green, like a smile carved into a puppet's wooden face. I caught myself twisting the rough homespun of my skirt with nervous fingers and forced my sweaty hands to smooth the coarse fabric. Many court ladies were stiff, I reminded myself.

Fresia did not make small talk. I did not mind, but she maintained an almost inhuman silence, making none of the little sounds people usually make, no sighs or sniffs, no idle scratching or bored nail picking. And sometimes, when I wasn't really looking at her, I felt an intent, almost predatory gaze upon me. Then I would look at her to find I had been mistaken, that she wore only that bland expression. Then she would smile like a wooden thing again.

Mostly, I stared out the window. The mind wanders at such times, and mine wandered to Halen. He would be semiconscious by now. Sam had likely found him.

After my being selected, the folk of Thistledown had broken into smaller groups, shocked and gossiping. Halen's absence had not been marked until then, for he rarely set foot in town, but his name had carried to me across the green as the coins had dropped into my hand. Those coins lay heavy in the pocket of my skirt now, a weight against my thigh.

The silver cloaks had closed around me and ushered me to the carriage. I had not looked back, had not peered between the silver waterfalls of cloth to seek out the eyes of any who had known me for seven years. Had it been pride? Fear? I couldn't be sure, but I regretted it as curiosity ate at me in the silence. I wondered whether Sam had been disappointed to see me go, or perhaps relieved.

Oh, what did it matter? I had never wanted that future. I would miss Prickle more than I would miss Sam.

I did not know if I would miss Halen. It was uncomfortable to think about him. How I had left him slumped at the table, his blacksmith's body too heavy for me to drag to his bed. How ill he would be right now. No, I would not think on that. I had poisoned him to save his life, as he had once burned me to save mine.

As the woods dimmed outside the carriage windows, the light drained from the interior until Fresia was little more than a shadow on the opposite bench.

We stopped suddenly. It was not the first stop. There had been a midday pause so I could duck behind a bush to relieve myself, emerging to find Fresia waiting nearby. She had given me that odd smile of hers before guiding me back to the carriage, where I'd found a silver tray of bread, ham, and cheese as well as a bowl of strawberries waiting on my seat. Fresia had watched me eat but had taken none for herself.

On this second stop, I expected we would make camp, but after I had relieved myself again, Fresia directed me back to the carriage. I halted at the bottom of the silver rungs. "We cannot possibly travel the night?"

"No. But you will sleep inside."

"And you?"

"You will want your privacy, I'm sure."

I did prefer that, but the arrangement was strange. She would camp with the men—and the Hunter?

I had caught sight of him at the midday stop. He had been ahead of the company, astride his black horse, and had not gazed back. I looked for him now, but Fresia gave me a little push. I climbed the rungs and ducked inside. A glass-faced lantern cast flickering light from the floor, and the silver tray, filled anew with supper, had been laid on one of benches. A pillow and blankets awaited me on the other.

The carriage door clicked shut behind me. Fresia appeared briefly at the window to close its shutters. Movement outside the other window caught my eye. I looked up to see the Hunter gazing in at me. The lantern's light licked at the underside of his jaw, casting shadows up his face, and his empty eyes were eerier than ever in the dimness. Eeriest of all, a rack of ghostly antlers rose from his head, trailing shadows like cobwebs caught in the tines. A faint light seemed to glow in their midst.

Some hint of feeling came into the Hunter's eyes. His lips parted as though he would speak, and the tips of his incisors gleamed in the lamplight. Then he scowled and slammed the window shut.

I stood there, bent under the carriage's low ceiling for a long, frozen moment. Then I reached out to test the window and found it locked. The other as well, and the door.

I sank down on the floor, shivering between the benches, huddling by the lantern. The enormity of what I'd chosen, of where I was, crashed down upon me. I was locked in an enchanted carriage in the middle of the woods, where faeries and strange creatures lurked. My safety rested in the hands of the queen's Fae and the queen's men—and nothing about that was safe at all.

But I had not chosen this for safety. And there was worse, far worse to come. There was Lyric.

If I wanted to be safe, I should have avoided the Selection as Halen had insisted, should have gone on with life in Thistledown after someone else had been chosen. I forced myself to picture the table in the cottage, not with Halen slumped against it but with me and Sam sitting across from one another, a platter of roast beef between us. Though I could conjure the scene, I could not picture my own face, not there.

Then I thought of that night in the Great Hall, of my father's blood and my sister's scream. I thought of all the years of my childhood, with Lyric a cool but unthreatening presence as Rose and I played and laughed. I thought of how long it had taken me to stop glancing to my right where Rose had always been.

———◆———

Most of the second day passed much like the first, time spooling out so unchangingly that I half expected to continue this way forever: my eyes numbed by the endless trees, Fresia silent and stiff across from me. I jumped with surprise, then, as we suddenly emerged from the woods onto a paved road. Lurching over to the window on the non-wooded side, I leaned out to see wheat fields and green pastures rolling along the road.

One of the guards stared at me, his initial surprise morphing into that unsettling hunger I'd seen before. I had forgotten the faces of the guards, so I wasn't sure whether this man was the same one who'd eyed me yesterday. I ripped my gaze away and looked ahead to where the Hunter led the way. Beyond him, a rocky outcropping blocked the view, but we had to be close to Orlas for the road to be paved.

Fresia let out a little hiss behind me, and I ducked back into the carriage.

"You must begin to think like a lady," she informed me.

We had not yet spoken of what it meant that I had been selected. I was supposed to believe I was destined for the life of a court lady. A marriage, mostly likely. I should have asked about what would happen in Orlas, even if I knew the answer would be a lie. Any normal girl would have asked.

"So that a fine lord will fall in love with me?" I could not keep the acidity from my voice.

Fresia gave me her wooden smile. "To please Her Majesty."

"I'm not to marry then?"

"Her Majesty will explain everything tonight."

My heart skipped. I would see Lyric *tonight*. What if she recognized me?

I cut that off. I had already settled the matter in my mind. She would not know me. Not seven years later. Not scarred as I was and coming from a remote village like Thistledown. Not if I lied well enough.

Yesterday, Fresia had said she would attend me in Orlas. I could think of no reason for her to lie about that when she could simply have said nothing. It indicated there would be some long-term element to the Selection. That was good. It meant there would be a chance to learn how things lay in the castle, to gather information, to look for opportunities.

There would be no wheedling information from stiff Fresia, so I occupied myself with the view, relieved by the sight of fields and grazing animals after the endless woods. I refrained from leaning out the window again, but I edged close to it for an angled look ahead.

I hadn't been in Orlas since I was eleven years old and had rarely traveled, so I wasn't familiar with the landmarks and wasn't prepared to sweep around a bend in the road and suddenly behold the castle's towers piercing the sky from atop the craggy tor.

I felt like those towers pierced my chest as well because my heart seemed to stop and the breath went out of me. Until that moment, I don't think it had been entirely real in my mind, what I was doing, where I was going.

My dread grew with every rotation of the carriage wheels, as the town spreading out below the tor like a rippled blanket resolved into hundreds of white-walled, slate-roofed buildings and the castle loomed ever higher. Had it always been so forbidding?

Though the road began to branch into the city, we stayed on the straightaway that cut between Orlas and woods. It took us to the switchback path up the tor, where the horses lurched into the climb. I glanced out to see, high above, how the queen's silvery banners had laid claim to the curtain wall.

We made the final turn, passing under the crenelated wall to reach the gates, where that color hung from the gate towers, the queen's five-point emblem starkly black against the shimmery backdrop. Her silver draped the shoulders of the cloaked guards who stood aside to let us pass.

The curtain wall contained an entire world, a city above the city of Orlas. Barracks and stables and workshops flanked the towering castle, and acres of lawn sprawled at its feet. Hedges lined our passage through it all. Somehow, I had expected desolation. Withered bushes, bare earth. Dust and ash. But she hadn't killed everything, apparently.

We emerged into the inner courtyard, and the carriage came to a stop. The door opened, and the Hunter appeared. It was my first close look at him since he'd scowled at me through the carriage window last night. There was no sign of his antlers now, and his face lacked expression, bearing only his unearthly beauty.

When Fresia rose from the bench, the Hunter withdrew to let her out. She frowned as though displeased, as though this was not his role. As I ducked out after Fresia, the Hunter caught my hand and guided me down. The gesture surprised

39

me nearly as much as what he pressed into my hand. A wad of cloth. I clutched it tight, understanding the secrecy of the transfer, resisting the urge to look at it. Fresia was watching me.

Why would the Hunter pass anything to me? What secret could there be between us?

I was almost glad of having the mystery to distract me during this moment of standing on my own shaky legs in the castle courtyard, on the cusp of discovering what trap I had, of my own will, stepped into.

"Come," Fresia commanded.

Clutching the wad of cloth in a tight fist, I followed her to the stone steps. At the top, guards in silver and black livery flanked the iron-braced doors.

As we climbed, I gazed up the castle's imposing front. It reared into the sky—a complex form of boxy walls and towers and crenellations of gray stone. Dozens of age-darkened statues jutted from its many faces and hundreds of windows stared out like black eyes. Here and there, the queen's silver banners hung with lifeless weight. At our approach, the guards pushed open the arched doors.

The doorway yawned wide like a gaping maw of stone, and as I followed Fresia through it into the entrance hall, I had the sense of being swallowed. *Inside the beast*, I thought as the ceiling soared overhead, ribbed with stone, and passageways branched off the hall like hollow veins. It was as cold as a witch's heart.

And silent.

It had never been silent before. In the beginning, when this space had been warm with sunlight or candlelight, my mother's voice had trilled through these halls. There had also been my father's deep rumble and Rose's sweet laugh, the easy murmurs of lords and ladies, guards and servants.

Later, there had been screams.

Now, however, there was only the tapping of Fresia's shoes and my boots. The sound emphasized how stilted her gait was, almost mechanical. She led me to one of the long hallways, where light filtered in from the high windows.

Then I began to hear whispers, wordless and drifting.

I stopped. Scanning alcoves and branching hallways, I glimpsed shadows that seemed to move without anything to cast them. Then, at the head of a hallway, a figure appeared as though gathering itself from the shadows. He wore fine court garments in silver and black but, like the guards, he had an unremarkable face—and that same intent look as he stared at me.

Fresia, who had kept walking, came back. She had acquired a candle somewhere.

As the man turned and walked away, Fresia gave me a stern look and said, "You're not to associate with anyone but the other girls. You must stay intact for Her Majesty."

"Intact?" My fist tightened on the wad of cloth the Hunter had passed to me.

"Pure," she amended, as though that were less disturbing. "Come along now."

As I followed Fresia deep into the castle, her candlelight licked the arching ribs of stone and shivered hauntingly over the tapestried walls. Had this dead, silent place ever been my home? It didn't seem possible.

Stairways whose destinations I couldn't recall took us up and up until we emerged into a fine hallway. Light bloomed from dozens of sconces, curving over graceful statues of stone and bronze and bringing out color in the tapestries. Though I hadn't recognized the route, I knew this hallway. It had once housed my mother's ladies. It surprised me so much that I almost said so and had to bite my tongue to hold back the words.

Judging by the doors we passed, several with light showing along their edges, this wing was occupied. By the other selected girls? Fresia stopped at one of the light-limned doors, an elegant panel of dark wood with a finely wrought brass handle. When she pushed the door open, warm light spilled out, and I followed her into a beautifully appointed chamber. In a hearth of pale stone, a fire crackled, painting a lighted invitation over the plush chair positioned before it and a copper tub full of steaming water.

Candles burned in silver holders on the tables, casting further light over a bed draped with red velvet and a grand wardrobe that reared toward the ceiling. The lush chamber befitted a highborn lady's maid. I had to sift past my years in Thistledown to see that. Coming from the cottage of a blacksmith, it looked fit for royalty.

I had half expected to be thrown in the dungeons, the Selection's lie revealed suddenly, the chosen girls betrayed instantly. To be brought here instead …

Lyric wanted the girls to believe themselves truly chosen, destined for a better life. Why?

"You will bathe," Fresia informed me. "Then I will help you dress for dinner."

"Dinner?" I seemed to have become a hollow thing, able only to echo her words in question.

After another of her wooden smiles, not answering, Fresia scuttled out of the room and pulled the door shut behind her.

I wanted to test the handle, to know if she'd locked me in this room as she had locked me in the carriage last night. But a more pressing question, clutched in my hand, demanded my attention.

4.

Magic and Malice

Though dirt had dulled the red flowers to the rusty color of old blood and the blue was darkened with grime, I knew my lost kerchief at once. I started shaking so hard that it tumbled from my palm. It fell to the rug with the same silence that had allowed it to escape Margret's hold after I had freed her from the faerie path.

I thought back to the day of the Selection, when the Hunter had moved along the line of girls on Thistledown's green. He'd paused before Margret, had looked back at her even after I'd struck him with my magic. Had he been trying to determine to whom the kerchief belonged? The only possible significance of that cloth was its presence in the woods, where I had worked magic. But I had already known he was aware of my magic, given my heavy-handed use of it during the Selection. The kerchief's return must be meant to communicate something else.

But what, I could not guess—nor could I let this mystery distract me. Fresia would be returning. I'd been instructed to bathe.

I snatched up the soiled cloth and strode to the fireplace, where I cast it into the flames. It flared and blackened and crumbled into ash.

The copper tub beckoned with its curls of rising steam, but I first made a circuit of the room, checking the shadows and hidden spaces. I found nothing but luxury. Cushions and rugs and a little silver bowl of chocolates, fine beeswax candles, a book of saccharine poetry. In the wardrobe, linen and wool hung in colorful abundance, and a few dresses even shimmered with the telltale luster of silk. The drawer below held stockings and delicate slippers and decorative boxes full of bright ribbons and hairpins.

The only thing missing was a mirror. It struck me as odd, that omission, but I did not mind the absence of my reflection.

After a last wary glance around the room, I removed my clothes as though removing armor, feeling more exposed and vulnerable with every inch of bared skin.

That feeling vanished as I sank into the blissfully steaming copper tub. My tense muscles loosened. My skin became my own again as I lathered it with the rose-scented soap I found in a little tray hanging from the tub's rim. I did not wash my hair because it would take hours to dry, instead letting the heavy dark locks trail outside the tub while I leaned back and sighed.

I must have dozed, lost in the dangerous luxury of warm water. As a whisper, light as a breeze, stirred in the room, I only half heard it. But it rose, as wind does, to a fierce and wordless sound, jolting me awake. I lurched upright, sending water sloshing over the tub's rim. The sound faded as I twisted about, hunting for its source, finding the sound everywhere and nowhere—then it was gone.

Every muscle the warm water had loosened seized with fresh tension as I rose to snatch up a waiting towel. Wrapping it around myself, I stepped out onto the sodden rug. That very moment, the door opened and Fresia walked in without so much as a knock.

Ignoring my startled indignation, she went straight to the wardrobe. Opening the doors, she flipped through the hanging gowns.

I squashed the temptation to reprimand her intrusion. A blacksmith's daughter spending her first night in a royal castle certainly would not.

After donning a linen robe that lay draped over the plush armchair, I went to see the garments Fresia had laid out on the bed. With a thin silk slip, a kirtle of pure white linen and an overgown of fine green wool embroidered with golden flowers, the attire befitted a court lady. Creamy wool stockings lay atop it, and a pair of burgundy calfskin slippers rested on the floor. The way Fresia had arranged it all, it almost looked like someone had lain on the bed and vanished, leaving only their clothing behind.

It made me wonder: had these garments belonged to one of my mother's ladies? Most had stayed on after my father had engaged himself to Lyric, hoping for a place with the new queen. I didn't know what had become of them. I didn't know what had become of anyone—the lords and ladies, the servants and guards. Did any remain here?

I stayed hidden within the robe as I rolled on the stockings, but I had to remove it to pull on the slip. My bare skin pebbled instantly, and I suffered through an embarrassing moment of nakedness with a stranger. Fresia was so impersonal, however, that it hardly felt like being with someone.

The kirtle skimmed my body, settling over my slight curves in an unnaturally perfect fit. Even the frocks I made for myself didn't fit so well. Fresia helped me with the green gown, lacing me into it at the waist and shoulders—another perfect fit. She tugged out puffs of the kirtle's white sleeves through the shoulder laces. I couldn't help the way I kept cringing away from her. I did not like being dressed. It had been too long and I'd grown used to my own space. She took no notice, so perhaps it was for the best that I acted on my discomfort. She would likely have been suspicious of a blacksmith's daughter who stood demurely, anticipating angles and holding up a foot or arm at the right moment.

Then again, I wasn't sure Fresia would have taken note of anything. She was so stiff and unfeeling.

When she tried to start in on my hair, I whipped it out of her hands. That was simply too much, too personal, with her hands so close to my face. She made no comment as I plaited the heavy dark locks myself, only handing me a red silk ribbon to tie the end.

The second I had the burgundy slippers on my feet, Fresia led me out into the hallway. We proceeded to the sweeping staircase, where light blazed at the top and bottom, gleaming along the gilded railing and rendering the carpet blood red.

Would she take me to the Great Hall for a formal dinner? My stomach churned at the thought.

But Fresia led me only one floor down, not to the Great Hall but to the royal wing's private dining room, where I had so often eaten with my mother and father and Rose. If Lyric had been in the room, I might have managed to remain cold and hard inside, but she was not, and a wave of unexpected grief sent me staggering into the sideboard, setting a wine bottle to rocking.

Candles burned in the crystal chandelier, casting twinkling light over the table with its ivory tablecloth and gold settings—just as I remembered. The paneled walls and blue velvet drapes, the flagstone floor, even the painting of my father's favorite horse—all unchanged.

Not really unchanged, though, for an unfamiliar girl sat in Rose's place. Plump and brown-haired, wearing a gown of purple damask over a yellow kirtle, the girl gaped at me. She clapped her mouth shut and looked to the girl beside her, a willowy blonde in pale blue who occupied my usual chair. Two more girls stared at me from seats on the other side of the table. One wore pink, the other deep orange. Like a jewelry box of girls. Their hair crowned their heads with braids and beads and glittering pins.

Their posture and poor nails gave them away, however, as did their uncertain glances at one another. Country girls in court finery. What game was Lyric playing with them?

With *us*, I supposed, for I had to join them and add my splash of green to the collection. Fresia's sudden clawlike grip on my elbow told me as much. I took a seat beside the girl in orange, putting my burn toward her—and toward where I expected Lyric would later sit at the head of the table. My father's place.

After I'd settled into my chair, Fresia left the room, closing the door behind her. The crystal wineglasses beside our bare golden plates stood empty. No servant appeared to fill them, and none of the girls had presumed to retrieve one of the bottles, nor any of the cheeses and cold cuts, from the sideboard.

The willowy blonde in pale blue was pretty, but there were no astonishing beauties among us. Still, beauty is always relative, and the blonde had clearly assessed herself as the fairest. Though she sneered at me, I could tell my scarred face was a relief to her. It would have galled her, perhaps, for a true beauty to walk in and bump her to second best.

"What is your name?" she asked with a superior air.

"I'm Gala."

"And you're from …?"

"Thistledown."

"Never heard of it. I am Vivianne, from Cottington," she announced, as though Cottington were a grand city and not a large town known for making glass. "This is Alice." Vivianne pointed to the plump girl in purple, who attempted a smile. "That's Beth to your right." She indicated the shy-looking girl in pink then waved a work-roughened hand at the slouching girl in orange. "And Sorsha."

"Did you all arrive today?" I asked. Alice's nod of confirmation seemed to annoy Vivianne, who clearly wanted to be in charge, but I ignored her. "So you haven't met … Her Majesty?" The words nearly stuck in my throat.

Vivianne gave me an unpleasant look that I took as a no, and Alice said, "I got into this room not a moment before you, right on Beth's heels. We don't know anything yet."

Casting a haughty look around the table, Vivianne observed, "I'm a little surprised." That we weren't beautiful, she meant.

Shy Beth shrank at the implication and Sorsha shifted uncomfortably, but Alice exclaimed, "No one was more surprised than me, I can tell you that. Why, when the, um, man?" Her voice fell to a whisper as she said, "The Fae." Her eyes darted around before she finished, "Why, when he picked me, I about fell on my bottom!"

The Hunter had picked her? But she had arrived only today? How was that possible when he'd been traveling with me, and from the farthest village?

"He brought you through the wood?"

Alice looked aghast. "Gods, no!"

"Did any of you travel through the wood?" They all looked at me like I was mad. "Did he select each of you?" Nods all around. "But he didn't travel with you?"

Vivianne interrupted the chorus of denials to demand, "What are you getting at? And what's your name again? I've already forgotten."

"Gala. And I was just curious."

I ignored her rude eyeroll. I needed to think. The Hunter had appeared at every Selection but had not traveled with anyone but me. He had devoted extra care to my arrival. Maybe it meant nothing except that Thistledown lay far away and he'd needed to catch us up. But he had returned my kerchief to me. Had he been saying that he'd felt the magic I'd worked in the woods, that he'd tracked that magic to the kerchief—and then to me? Specifically? Perhaps he had not so much *selected* me as *hunted* me.

I did not have a chance to follow that line of thought, for the door suddenly opened. Every head whipped toward it but mine. I froze.

I had angled my braid to the right, hiding not my burn but my unblemished side, the side facing Lyric as she swept into the room. I had seated myself to position the burn toward where she would sit, but I had not considered her entrance. Around the edge of my curtain of ebony hair, she would be seeing my fair side. Snow White's side. She would know me. I was frozen with fear of discovery—and sheer, simple fear of her.

Witch.

Murderess.

Aunt.

She was a silvery figure at the edge of my vision. Silver and auburn. While my dark locks echoed my mother's, Rose had shared her color with Lyric. A mere eleven months lay between the sisters in each generation. The darkness and then the dawn. At least, that was how Lyric had once described it.

She made a high, lilting sound of pleasure. "Good evening, my treasures."

Lyric flowed into the room like water, rippling her silver way … to me. Her elegant fingers drummed lightly on my shoulder. I lifted my eyes up the silver waterfall of her dress, all its diamonds glittering in the light of the chandelier. I reached the expanse of creamy skin that showed the subtle swell of her breasts—she had always been slight, like me—then the swanlike arch of her neck. Finally, I lifted my gaze to her sharply beautiful face and the silver-gray eyes that I remembered so well. They practically gleamed with intelligence and power and madness. A slender silver crown rested among her auburn braids.

Her red lips parted in a smile, revealing perfect white teeth. "Hello, my dear."

Terror spiked through me. She knew. *She knew.*

"Poor child," she purred, and those elegant fingers lifted from my shoulder to brush my scarred cheek. I could not feel it through the ruined skin, but I still shuddered. "Don't worry, dear one. Someone will want you for your heart."

Then she drew away and flowed on behind my chair, fingers trailing over Beth's hitched shoulders before skimming Sorsha's mousy locks. When Lyric reached the head of the table, she regarded us all with a benevolent smile that made my skin crawl. "My treasures, you must rise when the queen enters."

As we scrambled inelegantly from our seats, Lyric's smile turned indulgent. "Very good, my dears."

At a slight wave of her hand, Lyric's high-backed chair slid away from the table. As she sat, the chair tucked itself beneath her, eliciting a collective gasp of surprise. Lyric winked, playful, as though we were coconspirators, and made a gracious gesture for us to be seated.

Our glasses filled with wine, the blood-red liquid rising within the crystal in another, bolder display of magic. Lyric's magic was no secret, but the girls would not be used to seeing such things, not coming from Cresilea's towns and villages, where even the most minor witchcraft was worked only in secret.

Lyric let out a tinkling strain of laughter at the shock so evident on our faces, the others genuine, mine feigned. I knew she was capable of more—and worse. She clapped her slim hands. "My loves, what fun!"

This was something of the Lyric I remembered. The moments of mad playfulness, the woman who was almost sweet, the smile that could be so bright—and cruel. She had smiled, after all, as she drove the blade into my father's heart.

"Oh, drink, my funny girls! Enjoy, for this is the most wondrous of nights!" Lyric curled elegant fingers around the stem of her crystal glass and lifted it to her lips.

Like the other girls, I picked up my glass and drank. I thought of poison, of course. I thought of the way my mother had sickened and died so suddenly. I thought of Halen slumped at the table in our cottage. I did not like the parallel, and I did not like to drink what Lyric had poured by magic into my glass, but there was no choice.

The wine flowed across my tongue with a soft caress and gentle bloom of flavor. It had all the seduction of that warm bath, all the refinement that would never be found in Annette's cider at the Thistledown Inn—and I hated that I loved it.

By the time I set my wineglass on the table, food had appeared on the golden plates. Bright asparagus and creamed spinach, sliced beef crusted with cracked pepper, delicate bread and toasted almonds, chicken in an herb-speckled sauce. More food than I could eat, more flavor than I had experienced in seven years. I glanced at the other girls to see wonder on their faces. Beside me, shy Beth licked her lips.

"Napkins, my dears," Lyric instructed, like a governess as much as a queen. We mimicked her, taking up our silk napkins and spreading them across our laps. "Eat, my treasures, and I will tell you a story."

The table setting almost made me revert to the court manners my mother had taught me, but I stopped myself. A blacksmith's daughter would clamp onto her fork and knife like tools instead of fine instruments, and I must not reveal myself by forgetting that.

"Once upon a time," Lyric began as we made our first eager stabs at the exquisite food. "There were two sisters."

My heart leaped, thinking of Rose and myself, but the story Lyric told was her own. A version of it anyway.

"They lived a simple and beautiful life in a sweet little cottage on the shore of a lake. Every day, a pure white swan glided across the lake, whose water was as smooth and clear as crystal. Like a perfect mirror, the lake reflected the sky and all the trees at its edges and the beautiful swan that paddled so gracefully she never disturbed its surface.

"All day, the sisters would spin and weave or gather flowers or brew potions and play with magic. They delighted in it. And every night, the swan would step out of the lake and change into a beautiful woman—the most beautiful woman that ever lived. The reeds and grasses worshipped her finely shaped feet, and the moon sighed at her beauty as she walked to the cottage, where her two daughters waited."

Around the table, the girls' eyes widened. A piece of chicken fell from Alice's fork into the sauce on her plate, sending a splatter of white onto the sleeve of her purple gown. The splatter vanished.

Lyric's expression turned wistful, as it always had when she had told this story to me and Rose, whispering it in the garden, telling us that Mother didn't like to remember.

"So it was for many blissful years. Until one evening, mere moments before sunset, the lake reflected something new—

and unwanted." Lyric's voice hardened, and her lip curled as she went on. "A young king had been hunting in the woods nearby, as young kings like to do. He had evaded his party ... as young kings like to do. And when he came upon the quiet lake and saw the most beautiful and pure of creatures gliding across its crystalline surface toward the shore, he drew an arrow from his quiver and set it to his bow, and he loosed that arrow upon the fair and unguarded creature—*as young kings like to do*. His arrow struck the swan in the middle of her transformation, and it was not a swan but a beautiful woman who fell dead upon the lakeshore."

Tears spilled down Alice and Beth's faces, Sorsha had shrunk away from the story, and even Vivianne looked horrified. I struggled to keep my breathing even, for the story was true, in part. According to my father, however, my grandmother had not turned into a maiden. She was yet a swan when she died, and he had taken her to the cottage in offer for a night's shelter. I'm not sure, really, which version was worse.

"And what did the sisters do?" Alice asked breathlessly.

"Did they kill him?" Vivianne asked hopefully.

They didn't know that the story was about King Philip. No one knew that but Lyric and me and the dead. All anyone knew was that King Philip had returned from a hunting trip with two beautiful women, that he wed first one and then the other.

He had done it to make amends for his mistake. My mother was worth loving. But Lyric, whom he had brought along for the sake of his wife's peace and comfort ... Lyric, he should have left at the lakeshore.

"One sister was brave and had loved her mother," Lyric told us. "The other ... well." Lyric shrugged my mother out of the story. "The brave one killed that king."

"And then?" Alice pressed.

"Another king came along," Lyric said brightly, further diverging from the usual narrative, that eerie cheer returning to her voice. "King Philip." The girls gasped, and Lyric smiled. "And what a magnificent king he was, for he took the two sisters to his castle and wed one, and after she died, he wed the other. But the other was robbed of his love, for he was slain most foully on their wedding night."

Now the girls recognized the story, and they swallowed hard, food forgotten on their plates.

"Yes, my loves," Lyric purred, and her eyes shone with a sadness that made my heart twist with cold fury. "It is my story. I tell it to you—I entrust it to you—that may you know how I, like each of you, came from a small place. That is why you are here. Because I know your hearts. They are full of magic. But you do not have a swan maiden mother to teach you, and even if you did, the world is not safe for magic, not unless you are queen, not unless you are here. That, my loves, is *why* you are here."

Now the girls looked anxious, and I suddenly understood: they all had magic. Gods, how relieved I felt. Even if the Hunter had sensed my magic from a distance, it had not stood out uniquely. The Hunter had tracked all of us, had *selected* all of us, for the same reason.

"Here," Lyric went on, "you will be under my wing. You will learn, as you could not have learned in your little villages. I will teach you and enrich you, and when your hearts have bloomed with magic ..." Lyric's eyes gleamed bright as jewels, then her voice took on that cheery lilt again as she said, "Then we shall find you your perfect match. Won't that be wonderful, my darlings?"

The girls' eyes were fixed on Lyric, and the anxiousness left their expressions, replaced by cautious excitement—and awe. Lyric breathed deep, as though she could smell their budding reverence. I tried to match the other girls' expressions. I tried so very hard. Yet, Lyric's silvery eyes settled on mine, glittering with malice. No—I had imagined it. She was smiling that beatific smile and not looking at me at all.

"There is one rule, my treasures. Are you listening?" Vigorous nods all around. "Very good. Now. You are not to associate with anyone except me and each other. It must be *just us*. For we are the best of friends." I shivered. She had said that to me and Rose after Mother died. *We shall be the best of friends.* "Do you understand?" Lyric asked and was answered by another round of eager nodding. "Excellent."

At her smile, our golden plates vanished and little crystal goblets filled with puffed pastry, sweetened cream, and bright strawberries appeared before us.

"One last thing, my treasures." Five silver spoons paused, and Lyric smiled at us with benevolence as she said, "Don't wander at night."

5.

Bewitchment

Late in the night, I padded across my room's cool floor, unable to sleep without knowing why Lyric had warned us against wandering. Clad in the billowing nightgown that had been waiting on my bed after dinner, I set my fingers to the door's brass handle. I expected it to be locked as the carriage had been, so my heart skipped when the handle turned. I eased the door open.

The sconces had been extinguished, leaving the hallway dim and eerie with the faint moonlight that filtered in through a high window at the end of the hallway.

A wordless whisper breezed through the air, making the hair rise all over my body. I had once complained to my father of the whispers in this castle, which had begun after my mother's death. But my father had already been lost in grief and had only said that Mother was gone and that I should not pretend otherwise. But I had never mistaken the whispering voice for hers.

So fair, so fair, so fair, so fair.

I froze. I had never discerned words before.

Soooooooo ...

Faaaaiiiirrrrrassoooooo ...

So? Or was it *snow*?

As the whisper faded into the shadows, something else emerged from them. The dark figure moved with an awkward gait, somehow wooden, somehow scuttling, but at least it was a familiar strangeness.

"Fresia," I breathed.

Her head tilted slightly. "No. But I am here. You may call me Armesia."

Even in the moon's faint light, I could make out enough of her features to recognize the ones I had seen across the carriage for two days. And that gait. That voice ...

Her head tilted the other way. "Do you need something?"

"Er ... no."

"If you are sleepless, I can make something to help."

"No," I said quickly, fear spiking at the thought of a sleeping draught that would render me senseless and vulnerable. More vulnerable anyway, for I felt helpless as it was, there in my nightgown in the dark, speaking with this mirror image of Fresia.

"Sleep well." A smile seized her lips.

I closed the door, shutting that away and wishing suddenly for the very lock that I had so dreaded finding.

The next morning, the other four girls and I gathered around silver-garbed Lyric in the garden. Fresia had dressed me in a gown of dark blue velvet whose skirt split in the front to display a wedge of the gold satin kirtle beneath. Gold embroidery twined along the edges of the blue: flowers and birds and winding ribbons. I did not want to love it. I did not want to feel like I was, finally, myself again.

My winter child, Mother used to call me. *With skin as white as snow and hair as dark as the longest winter night—my beautiful winter queen.*

And yet ... I was not that, not seated as I was with the other girls under the apple tree, the five of us perched on our silk cushions around Lyric like five colorful little birds there to amuse her.

Even that I struggled to be, for nothing in this idyllic setting could ease my nerves, which were stretched as thin and tight as harp strings. When Fresia had entered my chamber at dawn, again without a knock, I had cringed away from her, my reaction strong enough to penetrate her insensitivity. She had drawn back and smiled woodenly, just like she had in the past. Just like her ... twin.

Clutching the bedclothes to myself, I had asked, "You have a ... sister?"

She had looked at me blankly.

"Armesia?" I tried.

"Yes. A ... sister."

Had I imagined the hesitation? I had thought so at first, hoped so—until Fresia had led me into the garden and I'd seen two more of them.

From atop her tasseled cushion under the apple tree, Lyric gazed around at the faces turned so ardently toward her.

Above us, the branches bent this way and that, gnarled and lovely and busy with small green fruits. My mother had loved this tree. She had loved every plant in this garden, all the beds that swept out around the orchard, the groomed paths between them. Lyric had always hated it.

Men made this, I had once heard her tell Mother. *Aria—how can you love what men have made?*

A man made my children, Mother had said.

Lyric had only scowled.

"Now, my treasures, today we begin your enrichment. Who has worked magic before?" When no one responded, Lyric tsked gently. "Come, now, darlings, we mustn't lie, and we mustn't be afraid. Magic is beautiful. Why should we hide our beauty?"

Lyric cupped her hands, and a red rose bloomed there, velvety soft and exquisitely fragile. She smiled at our gasps of delight. Then the rose turned into a scarlet bird that twittered and hopped to Lyric's fingertips before fluttering into the branches above.

"How fine!" Alice exclaimed.

Vivianne shifted forward on her cushion, shimmering in her amethyst silk. Her blonde hair crowned her head in an intricate braid. "I have … done magic."

Lyric gave her an encouraging smile. "Go on, my dear. What wonder did you work?"

"I … turned a handful of pebbles into coins. I didn't mean to. I stared at them and *wished*. I scarce believed it when they gleamed in my hand."

"And what did you buy, my darling?"

"A cake. With pink icing and candied violets."

Lyric clapped her hands. "Clever girl!" As though Vivianne had not robbed the confectioner. As though the coins had not later become pebbles once again. My mother had warned me and Rose about illusion. *It is seeming*, she always said, *a deception.*

But does it harm? Rose once had asked.

It can.

"I didn't do it again," Vivianne went on. "The confectioner claimed someone had robbed him with magic. Others laughed, but I could see they were afraid it might be true. I did not want to die for a piece of cake."

We all fell silent, even Lyric, all of us understanding. When people are afraid, they punish not the crime but the crimes they fear in the future.

"I once broke a teapot in my mother's shop," Alice confessed. "I was in terror of her finding out and wished desperately for the damage to be undone and ... then it was. A week later, a woman knocked that same pot from her table at the teahouse. It fell to the flagstones without shattering. Everyone stared. My mother laughed and said how lucky it was, but she took the teapot away. Mother scolded my sister, who cried and said she had no magic. Mother never even looked at me. She didn't think I could be capable."

"She did not see you," Lyric said sympathetically, "but I do."

Alice blushed and gazed upon Lyric with devotion.

Lyric looked to the rest of us, but shy Beth lowered her eyes. To buy myself a moment to invent a story, I mimicked her. I had enchanted a goat perhaps, to make it obey. Prickle had tempted me often enough.

Sorsha spared me the lie when she confessed, "One time … I cleaned all the stalls in my father's barn by magic."

Sorsha's reticence was not like Beth's natural shyness. Her slouching was neither sloppiness nor sullenness; she was a wary and guarded thing. Lyric seemed to sense that as well because she pressed, like a hound on a scent, "Only one time?"

Sorsha slouched in on herself and muttered, "Father was angry."

Lyric's nostrils flared, and the fury in her silver-gray eyes roiled like a thunderstorm. "Did he hurt you?"

Sorsha's silence was answer enough, as was the far too old look in her young eyes.

Lyric asked, "Shall we kill him, my love?"

"He … fell. Plowing. He fell on the blade." Sorsha whispered, tears spilling down her cheeks, "It was a terrible accident."

Like a river of silk, Lyric flowed over to Sorsha and curled elegant fingers under the girl's chin. Lyric caught each of Sorsha's tears and turned them into diamonds. Sorsha sucked in a breath as Lyric then took her hand and turned it palm upward and let the jewels fall, hard and glittering, into her grasp.

"Our suffering makes us stronger," Lyric breathed. "There is beauty in that."

Sorsha gazed upon my aunt with hope, such terrible hope. I felt more fear in that moment than I had at dinner the night before. Lyric had bewitched my father with magic, but she was bewitching the girls with love.

There are so many kinds of power.

"Magic lies here." Lyric pressed her hands to her own heart, against the silver velvet of her gown. "We find a truth within ourselves, and we make it real."

"Will we learn spells?" Alice asked.

"Yes, my darling." A leather-bound book appeared suddenly in Lyric's hands, and she cracked it open. "Spells help us focus, but never forget that the magic is not in the spell but in your heart. It is that which we must grow." Lyric turned the thick, stiff pages.

The spell book had come with her and my mother from their cottage by the lake, and Mother had used it to teach me and Rose, so I knew all the simple spells that Lyric taught us that day. I pretended to be clumsy and frustrated. My errors delighted Vivianne, whose blade of grass lifted higher than anyone else's.

Our lunch appeared: platters of braised fish, tureens of soup, and little sandwiches of cucumber and tangy goat's cheese. When a pink cake crowned with candied violets materialized, Vivianne squealed with delight at the grand version of the cake she had bought with her handful of pebbles. Lyric smiled indulgently.

I tried to seem as bewitched by love and gratitude as the others, as blinded by it, but I knew Lyric must notice my wariness, the way my eyes would snag on the other people in the garden, who were wandering the neat paths. I recognized some of them. Lord Ursen with his broad orange mustache. Lady Camille with her square jaw and slight limp. Everyone in the garden wore the same vague look I had once seen on my father's face. That alone would have been enough to chill me, even without the rest of it.

Their clothes bore years of stains and numerous tears that had not been mended. Lady Camille's parasol had a ragged gash that let the sun stream through onto her face. She did not seem to notice. Another lady wore only one shoe, and a man was having a conversation with someone who wasn't there.

In a flow of silver, Lyric appeared suddenly beside me. I jumped. My teacup bounced off its saucer, spilling tea onto my beautiful velvet gown. The stain vanished. And all those things I'd seen ... they were gone. The lords and ladies wore pristine, polished clothes. There was no missing shoe, and Lady Camille's parasol was bright and whole. The man talking to himself had a companion now.

"What big eyes you have," Lyric breathed.

"I ..."

"You're very special, my dear." Her elegant fingers trailed from my chin down my throat and all the way to my heart. "The fairest of them all."

As the weeks passed, Lyric spent a great deal of time with us, teaching with a patience that surprised me. I suppose it shouldn't have. She'd already proven her patience, waiting over a decade to strike at my father. Mad and malicious she might be, but she was calculating as well.

We spent many mornings in the garden, learning from the spell book until we could each create pretty little illusions and pour tea without touching the pot and shape soap bubbles from nothing. Is it awful that I enjoyed it? It brought so much back to me, calling up knowledge from faded memories. I told myself that every moment of practice was one step closer to my goal, but I could hardly expect to kill Lyric with a soap bubble.

And was that my goal, to kill her? There are so many more comfortable words: punish, remove, defeat. But they all came to the same thing.

Lyric deserved to die. She had killed my mother—in my heart I knew it, no matter that the physicians had called it a sickness in the blood. Whether with a toxin or magic, Lyric had poisoned her. And I had witnessed her murder of my father. And Rose ...

Rose, I could not think about. And yet, she haunted me. There was not a hallway I had walked without her, not a room without a memory. And Lyric's hair ... that *hair*.

Rose Red, my mother had called my sister. Her summer child.

When loss dug icy fingers into my heart, I knew myself capable of killing Lyric. I had the will—but not the power, and my slowly remembered childhood magic would not be enough. I needed allies. I recalled enough of my childhood lessons in governance to know that power was not held in isolation. Even Lyric's was not. Her allies might be unnatural, her power inexplicable, but it all formed a network of some kind.

But my accessible allies—the ragged nobles who wandered the castle grounds like ghosts—were of no use. I needed someone from outside, someone not in Lyric's thrall.

Hope grew with hints of war.

Cresilea's northern neighbor, Trevar, ruled by King Stefan, was pushing back against Lyric's territory, claiming land that had once been contested between Trevar and Pontille—Pontille being the kingdom that Lyric had blamed and subsumed for my father's murder. Perhaps the subjugated Pontillians and the Trevarians might reach a territory agreement—and unite against Lyric.

I had to be patient, as patient as she. I had to learn all I could about her: her magic, her weaknesses, her purpose with the girls, and above all, who—or *what*—was serving her.

I soon had my chance.

Sometimes, Lyric would summon one of the girls, usually Vivianne, to attend her. One night, she summoned me.

6.

The Face in the Mirror

I had spent many hours in the queen's antechamber—once my mother's, now Lyric's. I had grown used to the pain of seeing my mother's green velvet couch under the windows, where she had so often reclined with a book. I was able to sit with the other girls on the cushions that Rose and I had once sat on together and let the blizzard in my heart go as still and cold as deepest winter. But I had not, in all this time, entered the queen's private bedchamber—once my mother's, now Lyric's.

Now, answering her summons, I hovered outside it, not wanting to see how she had overwritten my mother here as she had everywhere else, not wanting this last space in my memory to be defiled.

But Lyric had taken this room like all the rest, whether my eyes beheld it or not. I knocked.

"Come in, dear one," Lyric trilled from within.

Entering, I dipped into a curtsy as Lyric had taught us. "Your Highness."

With her tall, slender figure wrapped in a dressing gown of silver and gold, Lyric stood beside my mother's rosewood vanity. A fringed silver shawl hung over the vanity's mirror, blinding it. Lyric was removing my mother's ruby earrings and placing them in my mother's jewelry box. In each earring, silver settings bound three rubies in a dangling line. I had always loved those on my mother, the red so bright against her fair skin, so brilliant amid her dark hair. Seeing them on Lyric today, I had thought only of drops of blood.

From sconces and candelabras, light glowed throughout the room, glittering through the rubies as Lyric transferred them to the jewelry box of smooth, pale apple wood. Within lay many lovely ornaments: silver and gold, diamonds and pearls, emeralds and brilliant sapphires. Lyric had been given plenty of jewels of her own over the years, but every day she wore my mother's.

She smiled at my curtsy and closed the jewelry box. "How fare thee, Gala?"

"Very well, Your Majesty."

"Blue suits you."

I gazed down at the moth-eaten gown of midnight blue silk, its illusion no longer deceiving me. My kirtle of threadbare scarlet peeked through at the lacing of the shoulders and bodice.

"It's beautiful, Your Majesty," I claimed, smoothing the tattered skirt as though it shone like a polished gem. She liked to see our delight in the luxuries she provided.

Lyric seated herself on the cushioned stool before the blinded vanity mirror, her lustrous hair an auburn cascade down her back. She held up a silver-handled brush.

I approached and took it with fingers that trembled slightly, hoping Lyric would read my unsteadiness as excitement in attending her so personally. I ran the bristles through her hair from the shoulders down. It was the first time I had touched her in these past few weeks, and the intimacy of it scraped along my nerves.

"You must start at the roots, my dear."

"Yes, Your Majesty."

"That's better," she praised as I obeyed. I kept brushing, smooth and even, focusing on the task as though she was not the woman who had driven a knife into my father's heart right before my eyes. Sometimes it surprised me, frightened me even, to find myself capable of such an act.

Was it my early education, returning? *A queen must be able to put her feelings aside*, my mother had so often told me. *She must think and act beyond herself, even in spite of herself sometimes.*

I hoped such noble cause lay behind my fortitude. Sometimes, I feared I was dead inside, that Lyric had killed part of me when she killed everyone else. I feared how much I was like her. Did I not pretend pleasure in all I hated? Had she not done the same for over a decade in this very castle?

Lyric reached forward and pinched the silver shawl between her fingers, tugging gently. The cloth slid down to pool on the rosewood vanity.

At first, the mirror reflected us: Lyric, beautiful and regal on the cushioned stool; me, wielding the brush. Behind us lay my mother's bedchamber with its sumptuous four-poster bed draped in scarlet and gold. Tapestries wove a story across the walls, the story of an enchanted swan, one cursed by a wicked man for not loving him. Light, dancing from a dozen surfaces, played with the room's shadows. The spell book lay on the bedside table as casually as a book of poetry.

At first, I managed to resist the urge to look at my own face. In all these years, I had never seen my reflection clearly, catching only fleeting, unwanted glimpses in still water or window glass. But there is a strange compulsion to look into a mirror that stands before you.

I looked.

The scar stiffened the left side of my face, hardened it like cooled wax. Though I had always known it tugged down my lip, I had never imagined it to look so grotesque, so lopsided. No wonder people cringed from me—I cringed from myself. No wonder Lyric had not recognized me.

"Poor child," she whispered. "He will pay."

It jolted me. "He?"

"It is always men who harm us."

My hand tightened on the brush's handle. *Not always.*

I lied, as I always did, "It was an accident," then tacked on a belated, "Your Majesty."

"Hmm."

Fear spiked at her skepticism. Did she know something? But she couldn't, not about this. She saw only pain, and looked for a man's hand in it. I made myself wield the brush again, letting the task consume my attention, willing my hands to stop trembling.

Soooooooo ...

I looked up, startled.

Darkness had spiderwebbed along the edges of the mirror. Lyric was gazing intently into it, her silvery eyes seeking past her own reflection to something deeper.

Faaaaiiirrrr ...

The mirror darkened like a light was dying, until the bedroom all but vanished from its surface, as though Lyric and I hovered in a dim and shadowy space within its frame. Yet, the light did pick out some things: a post of the bed, a woven swan's wing. And stone—as though a rocky, cavernous chamber overlay the bedroom, two places blending in the mirror.

Lyric's hand caught mine, startling me anew. "A thousand strokes, my love."

A sense of calm wrapped around me like a comforting blanket, and the image in the mirror brightened to what it should have been: Lyric and me, the bedchamber and the candlelight. Even as I sighed in feigned relief, I threw off Lyric's illusion like the poisoned cloak it was.

Here is a thing some don't know: a prickly exterior, like a thorn-covered wall you dare not climb, or hard eyes that can stare someone into retreat? These mask a deep terror. Of people. Of pain. I knew how to lie with my stillness.

So I ran the brush through Lyric's hair over and over, and when the mirror darkened, the illusion fading, I allowed no sign of notice into my expression.

The two images intermingled once more: the hints of the bedchamber and of the stony cavern.

Queeeeeennnnn.

"King," Lyric replied.

I dared not seek her eyes in the mirror. I kept brushing.

She is faaaiiirrr.

"Yes," answered Lyric. To me, she said, "Very good, my love. The sides too."

"Yes, Your Majesty."

At the edge of my vision, twin lights sparked in the mirror. Not lights—eyes. They glowed like coals. A face emerged: pale and angular, with painfully sharp cheekbones and thin, dark lips. I pretended to work a tangle from Lyric's hair.

Sofffft and white and fair and briiiight.

"She is mine. You cannot have her."

Traaaade.

"No."

A hiss came from the mirror, making the hair rise on the back of my neck.

Lyric's fingers drummed on the vanity. "What would you trade for her?"

My hand faltered then I made myself draw the bristles through her hair again.

One hundred yeeeears.

Lyric stilled. "She's worth so much? Why?"

Blood and blood and blood and blood.

"I see. You have given me much to think on, Kraxikel."

The creature—Kraxikel—hissed again within the mirror, and its eyes flared in the darkness. Lyric stood abruptly, auburn strands of hair snapping from the brush's tines. She flung the silver shawl over the mirror. Her hands trembled as she straightened it.

Lyric spun away from the mirror then looked startled, as though she had forgotten I was there. I stood frozen, clutching the silver-handled brush to my breast. Lyric's fingers, steady now, curled around mine.

"Can I tell you a secret, my love?"

I made myself gaze up into her eyes. She was taller than I, as tall as most men. I gave the slightest nod, not trusting my voice.

One of her hands moved to my scarred cheek. My skin prickled at the barely-felt touch and I repressed a shudder like my life depended on it.

Lyric's silvery gray eyes, calm and wholly rational, fixed on me. She said, "Gold is nothing. Silver is nothing. Jewels are nothing. There is only one currency in this life, and that is pain."

7.

Strange Encounters

There was to be a ball.

Lyric announced it in the dining room one morning while the five of us girls ate our crumpets and sipped tea sweetened with honey and mellowed with cream. One of us, she said, was ripe. No one else seemed troubled by the word.

Ripe meant ready.

Ripe meant chosen.

Ripe meant wedding.

To the other girls, at least. To me it meant *out of time*.

But time for what? I still had no idea what Lyric wanted with us. She taught us magic and manners. She positioned herself as our benefactress. If nothing else, these past weeks had shown me that Lyric was a complicated woman. Wicked and cruel and selfish, yes, but I sensed something genuine in her enjoyment of us. Could it be true that she was raising the selected girls to be devoted allies? Were the girls from past years sprinkled throughout Cresilea, a network of loyal witches? That idea offered cold comfort. Such a network could prove an obstacle to Lyric's dethronement.

Then there was the face in the mirror. Who was Kraxikel? What was he—and what was Lyric's connection to him? The others in the castle appeared to be in service to her, but Kraxikel had seemed different, more dangerous.

At Lyric's announcement, laughter and excited speculation tangled into a bramble of joy. Vivianne snapped her fingers, and a white lily bloomed between them. She had grown fond of finger snapping to announce her magic. Sticking the flower into her hair, she practically glowed under Lyric's smiling approval.

Lyric promised handsome men to dance with and a special honor for one of us, the girl whose heart was ready. At the pleading for answers—*oh, a hint at least!* Alice begged—Lyric offered only an enigmatic smile.

The coming ball meant no lessons that day. There was hair to be washed and scented, nails to be shaped and buffed, dance steps to be practiced with giggling absurdity as everyone darted to each other's rooms.

Alice swept into my room at one point, spinning so that the gauzy outer layers of her gown drifted around her, ragged and stained. Sinking into a lopsided curtsy, she grinned and said, "You look very fine, Gala."

I swished my moldy green skirts and played along. "Why thank you, my lady." I turned to Fresia, who had scarcely given me an inch of space all day. "Perhaps Alice and I might style each other's hair?"

Fresia's head tilted. "As you wish," she said but did not move. I would have no freedom from her today it seemed. Not that it mattered. Never had I caught a hint of doubt or fear in Alice's eyes, nor anyone else's. Never had my subtle questions, probing to see if any of the girls sensed Lyric's illusions, resulted in anything but confusion.

No one would escape because no one wanted to.

Alice sat on the footstool before the cold, empty hearth in my room, twittering on about the ball while I braided her hair as best I could. Alice fiddled with her necklace, not noticing the empty setting where a jewel once had been.

I knelt before her as though to see how the style looked, aware of the unblinking statue that was Fresia in the background. "So you really think one of us will find someone to wed?"

She gripped my hands. "Her Majesty will see it so—for *all* of us." Sympathy warmed her eyes. She was thinking of my scarred face. I smiled stiffly and pulled my hands away.

As I descended the grand staircase that evening, holding my skirts above my slippered feet, my path converged with that of Lady Camille.

"Good evening," I said, earning a sharp look from Fresia at my side.

Lady Camille gazed at me with dull, unfocused eyes. Her sallow skin sagged like a much older woman's, and she looked as worn out as the yellow ball gown that hung by a single strap. She opened her mouth, revealing rotting teeth, and emitted a string of incoherent syllables.

"*There you are.*"

The words rasped like cloth against stone, and I turned to see a male dressed in black, with silver embroidery sparking along his lapels, eyeing me intently as he approached. At Fresia's hiss, he shifted his gaze to Lady Camille, holding up an elbow. She rested a gloved hand upon it. Ragged fingernails protruded from several frayed fingertips.

I shivered as they drew ahead of us.

"You are to speak with none but the other girls and Her Majesty," Fresia reminded me sharply.

"Of course."

Fresia led me to the Great Hall, the huge, beautiful room where my father's court had once celebrated every festival with food and music, where I had once danced with my father by standing on the tops of his feet as my mother swung Rose around in a silly parody of courtly dance. Where, later, my father sat on the dais with Lyric and gazed at her with his bewitched eyes. Where, that night, they danced together, sailing around the stone-paved floor until she drove a knife into his heart and he fell at her feet in a pool of blood.

Candles and torches flickered throughout the vast space, and a fire roared in the massive hearth. Being midsummer, so much flame should have made the Hall stifling hot, but the air remained cool, as it always did in the castle. The flames danced with the shadows, somehow in harmony with the high, eerie music drifting from the dim musicians' gallery.

Beth arrived and offered me one of her shy smiles. I tried to return it.

Leaving our unblinking attendants behind, Beth and I walked to the dais, where Lyric sat in my father's high-backed chair in a gown of silvery gray, her auburn hair pinned up under a gleaming silver crown that spiked high like inverted icicles.

From the long tables bracketing the dancing space, dozens of figures in black and silver watched our passage with hungry expressions. Among them sat the remains of the court: Lady Camille and so many others. Some sipped from goblets or nibbled at delicacies. Others slumped like dolls that had been plunked down at a child's tea table. The dark figures petted and sniffed at them. One ran a long, tapering tongue up a lady's cheek.

If I let myself relax, I could see the illusion: fine gowns and bright-eyed lords and ladies, all chatting and laughing, the dark figures unnoticeable and unthreatening. Beth and I joined the others on the dais.

There was dinner, dizzyingly rich.

There was music, with strings and flutes whose shrill notes made my scalp prickle.

There was Lyric, smiling fondly at us as though she had not murdered my father twenty feet away.

Then there was Lyric standing from her chair and saying, "My dear Vivianne," and offering her hand—and Vivianne lighting up with pride and joy as she placed her hand in Lyric's and the two of them stepping down from the dais.

"Come, girls," Lyric called, and we followed. She told us, "You must dance with none but to whom I hand you. Do you understand, my treasures?"

Oh, yes.

Of course, Your Majesty!

Oh, yes, oh, yes, oh, yes.

A tall, handsome man in a silver uniform appeared in the open space between the tables. Lyric bent to press a kiss to Vivianne's cheek, then she handed her off, and smiling Vivianne sailed into his arms, and he swept her into a dance.

But he was an illusion of Lyric's. Vivianne was dancing alone.

We all danced alone, handed off by Lyric to dreams and fancies, spinning through light and shadow to the eerie music.

Then the others swarmed onto the dance floor, all those inhuman things and the hollowed-out members of the court. They scuttled and tripped around us, but the girls laughed and smiled and didn't notice. Voices scraped and slithered at us.

"*May I taste you?*"
"*Might I try you?*"
"*Just a bite?*"

Vivianne glowed brighter and brighter until her magic overflowed to spill flowers and jewels and silk ribbons from her fingertips and lips, all of it tumbling in her swirling wake. Illusion after illusion of tall, beautiful men courted her and when the handsomest offered himself in a low bow before her, Vivianne dropped into a curtsy. The man offered his elbow and Vivianne laid her fingers upon it.

Chin high with pride, cheeks flushed with pleasure, she swept out of the Great Hall, fingers perched on empty air, and Lyric trailing behind her.

In Lyric's absence, Fresia and the other attendants peeled out of the shadows to keep watch over us. I had to whirl and dip my way to the edge of the hall. I spun illusions of my own and left an empty image of myself behind while I bled into the shadows. I did not know how long my tricks would last, but I hoped it would be long enough.

My flight up the red-carpeted staircase brought me breathlessly to Lyric's door. I had slipped a table knife up my sleeve at dinner. An absurd weapon against Lyric, but it felt better than empty hands. My smattering of spells would be of little more use, but I had to try.

The door to her antechamber stood open, and I slipped through, hiding myself in the shadows, grateful for the silence of my soft-soled dancing shoes. The bedroom door stood open as well. My eyes swept the empty chamber, where a single lamp burned at Lyric's bedside. The spell book, which had lain there when last I entered, was gone.

White as snoooowwww ...

I nearly jumped out of my skin.

When nothing sprang from the shadows, I crept to the vanity and drew the silver shawl aside a few inches to peer at a sliver of the mirror. A pale hand splayed across it as though it were a pane of glass. The spiderlike fingers were too long, had too many joints, and were tipped with sharp, black claws.

So frightened?

When I could make my fingers work, I pulled the silver cloth free of the mirror and let it pool on the vanity. Kraxikel's eyes glowed like coals in his pale, angular face, and his black lips drew into a smile that revealed sharp teeth.

Hello, fair one.

Darkness had crept in from the mirror's edges. Kraxikel and I seemed to hover in a shadowy space where pieces of two worlds coalesced.

In the mirror, Kraxikel slid behind me. I spun, but the room lay empty at my back, the candle yet burning peacefully on the bedside table. Whipping toward the mirror again, I found him behind me in the reflection.

Not real, I told myself, but when his spidery, clawed hand curled over my shoulder in the mirror, I felt it like a physical touch. A shudder racked my body, and Kraxikel smiled, displaying his jagged teeth. His eyes locked on mine in the framed glass.

Did you come to me for death and vengeance? I can give it to you. Anything you want. Everything you want.

I stilled. Did he know who I was? *White as snow*, he'd said.

What will it be? The power to destroy her? The power to save the others?

"What are you?"

His black lips stretched back from his sharp teeth. *You haven't guessed?*

I shuddered. Deep down, I knew. Deep down, I had known for a while. I stared into those hellfire eyes and demanded, "And what do *you* want ... demon?"

That sharp smile again—and no answer. Then: *I would bring your sister back to you.*

It stopped my breath. For the briefest moment, my eyes saw not Kraxikel but his promise. Rose, smiling and bright, warm as the summer dawn.

But she was gone.

Everyone was gone.

As the demon's promise curled around my heart, I hardened it to ice and let it shatter all over again.

So strong, Kraxikel marveled and stroked my ruined cheek. As his spidery, claw-tipped fingers brushed the tight and pitted flesh, it melted into creamy smoothness and transformed my face into a single, unblemished whole.

I stared and stared as he faded from the mirror, coal-bright eyes winking out. The truth returned painfully: my mother's room, now Lyric's. My face, ruined.

I gazed down at my moldy green dress. This was reality. My scar was reality. Lyric taking Vivianne was reality. But how could I guess to which of a hundred rooms Lyric had taken her?

Or perhaps she hadn't taken Vivianne to a *room*.

Memory guided me through the castle to another possibility. My father had brought me here once, that I might know the ugly side of power. With a candle I had taken from its holder, I headed down a chilly stairwell, the candle's tiny light licking into the darkness and the table knife held in my other hand. At the bottom of the stairs, the heavy, iron-braced door was locked, but that presented only a moment's obstacle. The more I had practiced magic with the other girls, the more that had surfaced from childhood. Lyric, certainly, had not included unlocking spells in her lessons.

The dungeon was black as pitch. My candle cast a feeble ring of light on the dusty floor and brushed weakly over the iron bars on either side. Empty. Of course it was. Lyric had no need to bar in what she could bewitch. Chiding myself for foolishness, I turned to leave.

"Who's there?"

I spun, yelping as hot wax spilled onto my hand. I dropped the candle, which extinguished as it hit the floor. I extended my knife into the darkness, barely daring to breathe. "Who—"

At my feet, the candle relit.

"What are you doing down here, girl?"

After a wary glance at the candle, I picked it up and followed the gruff voice to the farthest cell, where a wizened little creature huddled in the corner, a long, white beard draping over its drawn-up knees. He wore a dirty red cap with a long tassel and stared at me from shrewd dark eyes that were nearly hidden under bushy white eyebrows.

"Why are you in here?" I asked.

I'd never heard of his kind venturing into Cresilea or any other human kingdom. Dwarves kept to their mountains, mining and crafting with their strange magic.

"Why are *you*?" he returned.

"I lost my way," I lied. Just because he was Lyric's prisoner didn't mean I could trust him.

He scoffed. Then he got to his feet. I stepped back at his approach, expecting his hands to curl around the bars. Instead, his nimble fingers played with the wiry strands of his beard. He wore a dirty, threadbare tunic that might once have been blue, and suede trousers that hung loose. The tassel of his red cap draped to one side, and tufts of white hair peeked out from under it. His feet were bare.

He said, "Blood she'll take and bone she'll break—but love she'll never give you."

"What does she want with you?" I demanded.

"The strength of a mountain in a silver ring. A crown for a queen—to stay a king."

I grimaced. "You speak in riddles."

Though the top of his head reached no higher than my waist, the dwarf seemed to look down his crooked nose at me. "I speak in truths beyond your reckoning."

"Not entirely. I do not look to Lyric for *love*." Something in me revolted at the word. "Tell me plainly why you are in here."

The dwarf stroked his beard and seemed to consider me seriously for the first time. "No cobwebs adorn your eyes. Who are you, girl?"

"No one that need concern you."

"I disagree, Burned One." Starlight seemed to glitter in the dark depths of his small eyes. "You stand at my door. Let me out—and I will let you in."

"I don't want in." I tacked on, "Shriveled One."

"You will."

Absurd creature. I had no desire to enter that cell or any other.

His nimble fingers played his beard like a flute. "When the cold bites your bones. When the stones groan and the wind moans—you will."

"More riddles," I complained.

His dark eyes studied me, twinkling more brightly, mischievous. "She is more cuckoo than songbird."

"Speak plainly."

"Dull-witted girl. The cuckoo takes the nest and accepts that which is given, but in blindness."

"And that is plain speaking?"

"She would rule more than she has power for. She looks to others for it."

"I am well aware of that," I snapped, thinking of the mirror and Kraxikel, annoyed with the dwarf's word games.

"You are wary but not aware."

"I'm wary enough to leave you where you are."

"You will let me out."

"Why don't you let yourself out?" He had magic, after all. "Is it the iron?"

He ran a hand up one of the bars. "Bones of the mountain break and make at my touch—if the forge be fired."

I turned as though to leave him. "I tire of your games."

"You shiver, child, even at the small fire I took from your blood to light the candle. Maybe all the ice in you would shatter these bars—or maybe not."

I halted, suddenly aware of the chill in my blood. I had thought it fear. "You took something from me to work your magic?"

Those small, dark eyes glittered. "I am a crafter of things. I shape and remake."

"And that's what Lyric wants from you?" I asked, beginning to make sense of him.

"As I said."

"A crown for a queen?"

He smiled under his long, crooked nose, which looked like a half-melted icicle that had refrozen in an odd shape. He looked pleased, though, like I wasn't as dull as he'd claimed. He repeated, "To stay a king."

"Stay as in *remain*, or stay as in *stop*?"

"Clever girl," said the dwarf. "Both, of course."

I frowned. "So she would stop a king and remain one?"

"Is she not queen and king in one?"

"I suppose." She had no husband, after all; she had killed him. "And the king she would stop ... Kraxikel? But she is the very one in allegiance with him."

"What makes the difference between ally and enemy?"

I thought back to my father's lessons. There were a hundred answers to that question, but I needed to think as

Lyric would. "Strength?" I guessed then remembered the dwarf's earlier words. "The strength of a mountain in a silver ring. She wants a crown to protect herself from Kraxikel?"

The dwarf's eyes twinkled. "A circle holds itself—things without and things within."

I took that as a yes. "And you refused?"

He gestured to the cell to behind him. *As you see,* he seemed to say.

I narrowed my eyes, not ready to trust him. "How did you come to be here?"

"Greed," he answered, plain for once, then added obliquely, "A mine shaft, a mountain path, a darkness neverending."

I grimaced. "Riddles again."

"I am a dwarf."

"Gods spare me from your kind."

"But the gods are not kind," he replied, reordering my words, remaking meaning.

"I noticed," I said grimly and slid the table knife into my sleeve so I could set my hand to the lock. It clanked open, and I hauled at the gate. "Come with me."

The dwarf surprised me by hesitating. "Someone will bear the blame. And with it, the pain."

"That is always the way of things. Come."

I had failed Vivianne, but I could still aid someone tonight. Besides, if the dwarf had power that Lyric wanted, then I wanted him as far away from her as possible.

Our route through the castle was not easy. I didn't know every hallway and had to backtrack to familiar ones in order to find my way to the door that opened onto the garden.

Demons lurked everywhere.

When silence was not enough, I wove illusions to distract them while the dwarf and I slipped from one hallway to another. It helped that they weren't looking for me. They were busy feeding.

The demons looked roughly human, except for their inhuman paleness, their skittering movement, and the long, awful tongues that roamed over the slack faces of the bewitched lords and ladies of the court. Sometimes I caught a glimpse of a long-fingered hand with black claws.

Lord Ursen, his orange mustache drooping, his skin dry and papery, slumped against the statue of a warrior on the castle's ground floor. He moaned as though a woman was at his throat instead of a demon. The creature breathed in Lord Ursen's scent. More than his scent, I suspected.

"You cannot help him," the dwarf whispered when I paused.

"I cannot help you both, you mean."

As a familiar, stiff figure emerged from a room, I hauled the dwarf into an alcove that housed a bust of my great-grandfather. I drew out the shadows, wrapping them around us like a cloak. As Fresia's footsteps drew near, I dared not even breathe.

I stared at her unblinking profile as she walked by, never glancing our way. I sagged, squashing the dwarf. I was about to apologize when he pinched me. I glared at him instead.

We made it to the garden, slipping from the castle into the night. Clouds veiled the stars, and the garden lay dark around us. Having left my candle behind to avoid attention, I now had to pick my way blindly through the orchard to the bramble of rosebushes. The canes snagged at me with seven more years of growth than last time. I was bigger now, too, and leading the way. By the time we reached the low, hidden gate, my hands stung with scratches.

At my spell of unlocking, the gate swung open. My eyes had adjusted, so I could pick out the first stretch of the rocky path down the tor. The woods at the bottom looked like a mass of shadow.

The dwarf paused in the gateway to cast one last riddle at me. "All must yield their heart, one way or another. Choose well."

"I think you riddle simply to annoy me. Is that my thanks for your liberty?"

"A riddle is a lesson that you learn when you're ready," he replied in his gruff voice. "Do not blame me for your own ignorance. I have many riddles and many truths with them—that is the true craft of the dwarves. Remember that."

With that, the infuriating creature was gone, moving quickly and silently down the path, lost to darkness in seconds. I closed and locked the gate then backed my way out of the thorns.

A faint light suddenly cast my shadow before me, as though the moon had emerged from behind a cloud. I turned—and leaped back into the brambles.

"Gods!"

The Hunter towered over me. Scraps of shadow clung to his antlers, drifting around him and partially obscuring the light that glowed amid the tines. Even so, enough light filtered down onto his face to paint its eeriness over his beauty. His eyes gazed at me with no hint of feeling.

Caught in the rosebush, frozen with terror and awe, not a single spell came to mind, not even as he reached for me. I expected an iron grip, but his hand closed gently on my elbow. The brambles loosened. As the Hunter pulled me free, the chill the dwarf had given me eased from my limbs, and the sting vanished from my scratched hands.

When I was on my feet, the Hunter let me go. He wore his green tunic, and a breeze played with the soft waves of his hair. His tipped ears peeked through, adding to his otherness. Yet, as unearthly as his beauty was, there was much of the earthy woodland about him.

"No," he said, the word rasping out like iron shedding rust. His eyes seemed to darken. His jaw clenched. He said again, "*No.*"

I shivered, chilled once more. No, what?

He shook his head slowly, and his lips pulled back from his teeth in a silent snarl. I shrank from him, but he made no move to seize me. Then he turned and began to walk toward the castle.

If I fled, would he pursue me? I could take the path as the dwarf had done and try my luck in the woods. But what about the other girls, and what about my purpose here? If I abandoned them, what had been the point of any of this?

So I followed him, the Queen's Fae, with the moonlight glowing amid his antlers and the shadows trailing him like cobwebs. He would take me to Lyric, I was sure. If he did, perhaps I could yet help Vivianne.

We entered the castle, and he led me not to Lyric but to my room. The door swung open, and I walked past him to scan the chamber. Fresia was not there. No one was. I turned to face him, puzzled. Why had he not taken me to Lyric? And why had he not stopped the dwarf's escape, which he must have witnessed? And my scratches—they were healed. *He* had healed them.

"Why?" I asked, at a loss for a more specific question when there were so many to choose from, but I think I was mostly asking, *Why do you serve her?* I saw none of the slack incomprehension of the bewitched lords and ladies. There was some other reason he did Lyric's bidding, and it was such a perversion of his wild beauty, of the fierce independence of the High Fae.

The Hunter opened his mouth as though to speak, but he made only a small sound that might have been frustration or anger or pain—then the door slammed shut in my face.

8.

The Apple Tree

Trevarian emissaries arrived the next day.

I had spent the remainder of the night making plans. How I would try to countermand Lyric's illusions and show the others the truth. I must make them afraid enough to save themselves. And the spell book—I would steal it when the time came. We would escape, all of us. Armed with knowledge of Lyric's ambitions, fortified with the promise of more power held in the spell book's pages, I would seek allies abroad, for there were none to be found here.

Even when the Trevarian company arrived, I thought, *Good.* I thought, *Opportunity.* I thought perhaps I could get a message to one of them.

Alice, Beth, Sorsha, and I stood with Lyric at a high window as the blue- and yellow-garbed soldiers dismounted in the courtyard below. Lyric's skin practically glowed, like she had bathed in milk and honey. Lyric had always been beautiful, but sometimes I wondered if she now used magic to perfect herself. She looked more like my older sister than my aunt. She said nothing of Vivianne, only smiled indulgently as Alice twittered to the rest of us about how happy Vivianne had looked.

Vivianne, I assumed, was dead.

To what purpose? Only one possibility seemed likely, and it was too awful to contemplate at the moment, in my present company. I needed a clear mind and steady hand to act my part around Lyric.

Her gaze lingered on me no more than on the others. My activities after the ball had gone unnoticed. Except, of course, by the Hunter.

Lyric gazed down into the courtyard with hard eyes. "The Trevarians would steal from us. Isn't that terrible, my treasures?"

She petted the closest girls, Alice and Sorsha, to soothe them when we all made sounds of dismay. Sorsha especially gravitated toward Lyric, leaning into her touch as she had not in the past. Vivianne had demanded the most attention, and Sorsha had spent the last month watching from behind her mousy hair, keeping quiet as she learned, enduring Vivianne's condescension. She must have done the same for years with her father.

"Do not fret, darlings. I would never allow anyone to take what is mine." She added in a barely audible whisper, fingers threading through Sorsha's hair, "Never again."

When Lyric left us to deal with the emissaries, the other girls wanted to go to the gardens. I suggested we go to the stable instead.

"I don't think Her Majesty would like that," Beth worried.

I shrugged. "Why not? She never forbids us anything."

Alice frowned. "We're not to speak with others, Gala, you know that."

"Why shouldn't we though?"

"Her Majesty said so."

"But why, do you think? What is wrong with talking to others?" I hated the sound of my own voice, the false lightness, the carelessness and ease. I did not realize until that moment how relieved I had been to speak with the dwarf, to not have to pretend. I would take his gruffness and riddles any day if I could at least respond as my own self and not as complacent, stupid Gala.

Sorsha looked intrigued, and Beth looked to Alice, whose frown deepened as her fingers played nervously on the casement.

"Besides," I went on in a light, teasing tone, "Do horses count as 'others'?"

Alice smiled a little. She was too good-natured to frown for more than a moment. "Well, I shouldn't think so, but—"

"But what?" I sighed dramatically and swayed into a dance step as though caught up in the memory of last night's ball. "I'm tired of the garden. Wasn't it nice to do something different?"

I would go alone if necessary, but my trip would be less conspicuous with the others. Lyric might see it as a girlish adventure, something to scold perhaps, but nothing more. And if any of the Trevarians remained in the stable, perhaps the sight of a few ordinary humans would do the girls some good.

In the end, they went with me, no one noticing how well I knew the way, all of them finally caught up in the novelty of it, twirling through remembered dance steps, setting dust motes swirling as we ventured away from our usual routes. They wanted to please Lyric, but she had not explicitly forbidden us from wandering during the day, and she had never punished any of us, her hold as light as though we were little birds.

A royal stable is usually a lovely place: clean and airy, full of well-bred horses, their coats brushed to a high gloss. The horses in Lyric's stable, however, were unnatural, hungering beasts. Dull, sparse coats stretched over their skeletal bodies. Scraggly manes hung down emaciated necks, and their eyes stared out dry and dull. Gooseflesh tightened my skin. These could not possibly be the horses I had seen in Thistledown.

But they were. When I relaxed and unfocused, I saw Lyric's illusion. It nearly made me vomit to think that these wretched animals had been the ones pulling the carriage I had ridden in for two days. They looked more dead than alive. By contrast, the Trevarian horses skittered in their stalls, wide-eyed and frightened, their flanks trembling, sweat running down their bodies.

This, I would show the girls.

I would rend this false weaving with cold, hard truth. I would try at least; I had never attempted such a thing.

"Gala."

I spun at the whisper, shocked by the familiar voice, so out of place here—and so dangerous. "*Halen.*"

Dressed in a Trevarian uniform, he beckoned me from an otherwise empty stall. My eyes darted to the other girls, who were feeding carrots to one of the skeletal black horses, unaware of the way its desiccated lips had shrunk back from its teeth, oblivious to the carrots falling, uneaten, into the straw.

I wove an illusion of my own, an image of myself with another of the horses, occupied with braiding its forelock, while I hurried to Halen, hissing under my breath, "What are you doing here?"

The blue and yellow uniform hung on his once-robust frame, all his blacksmith's strength leached away by whatever he'd been doing this past month. Riding to Trevar, it seemed. More gray showed in his sandy hair, and his careworn face looked ten years older. "We have to go."

After casting another look at the other girls, I slipped into the stall and crouched out of sight. "I cannot leave."

Halen crouched too, his knees cracking. Though barely a foot apart, we did not touch. He said, "King Stefan will hide you."

I meant to go to the Trevarian king but not until I had something of value to bring him—other than myself as a hostage. With nothing at the moment to make me valuable but Lyric's interest in me, he would use me as a piece in his own game, a token to trade if the brewing war did not go his way. That was one reason I needed more information—and the spell book. I had to be worth more as an ally than as a bargaining chip.

"You know how he would use me," I whispered harshly. Halen might not have been schooled in governance as I had been, but he was no fool.

"Better than being here," he insisted. "And we could flee if necessary."

Is that always your answer? I bit back the question and asked instead, "King Stefan knows of me?" I didn't like the idea.

"Yes." Seeing my reaction, Halen added, "The emissaries do not. Stefan is wiser than to share such valuable information. No one will reveal you to Lyric."

I shook my head, moving past that. "Stefan is badly outmatched. Lyric has ..." I hesitated. If I told Halen the truth, he would be even more determined to get me away from here. And yet, someone needed to know, to be able to carry the information away. Just in case. "She has allied herself with demons."

Halen's careworn face drained of color. "Then we must not wait. The path down the tor—"

"I won't go to Stefan as a beggar seeking shelter. He would only keep me to use me."

"Then we flee. Over the mountains. We go where she cannot find you."

"I do not understand you at all. You value me for my blood but do not seek to use it." Even *I* sought to use it. Without using it, it *had* no value.

I could still picture myself walking beside my father along a street in Orlas, a contingent of guards and servants in our wake. I could still hear him saying, *From your mother, you inherited beauty. From me, privilege and responsibility.* Seven years in a blacksmith's cottage, seven years as Thistledown's unwanted burned girl had taught me well enough that no value mattered outside of its context.

Halen blinked. "I ... That is not why I value you."

"It's what you said. In Thistledown. When you said I was the rightful queen." Those might not have been his precise words, but that was what his words had added up to. That was why I'd been able to dismiss them. It was why I'd been able to poison him.

I rose to peer over the edge of the stall. The girls had moved to another horse, but they showed no sign of noticing anything amiss.

When I returned to my crouch, Halen said, looking uncomfortable, "It was easier to say that than the hundred other things that I don't know how to say. I ... I am not good with words."

"It doesn't matter," I lied. "I don't care."

In truth, I craved words from him. I had since I was eleven years old and trembling in my court finery as we fled, as my sister's scream echoed in my ears and the image of my father's blood hung before my eyes like a mirage. Words have power. But Halen had none to give, and neither did I, so we both looked away, powerless.

Then, finally, he did find some words, and whispered them: "I cannot see past it."

My scar, he meant. I knew from his tone—and because no one could see past it. That had been the point. It stung to hear those words, even though I knew he meant that he couldn't see past his own hand in it. Was it as clear in his memory as it was in mine? The campfire. The iron pan. *Don't look, Snow.*

I said, "It was necessary."

"I thought so at the time, but I have questioned it every day since—and have hated myself every day since."

"It was necessary," I insisted. We both needed it to be true. Then I focused resolutely on the present. Halen and I could run out of time at any moment. "I won't flee to nowhere and I won't go to Stefan emptyhanded. Without something to make me valuable as more than a coin to trade, I would be no safer in Trevar than here, not for long. And I will bring those girls. Lyric is ... I think she is feeding them to the demons."

Halen shook his head. "Saving them will not bring Rose back."

I reared away as though struck. "That has nothing to do with this."

"Three girls are not worth—" We both froze at the sound of them moving this way.

"Gala?" Alice called.

I called back, "I dropped something in the straw. I'm coming!" To Halen I whispered, "I won't leave without them." I made my tone final, as I had heard my father do so many times.

Desperation flashed in Halen's eyes, but there was no time to argue. He whispered hurriedly, "The Trevarians leave tomorrow. Bring the girls if you can—but get to the bottom of the tor. *Please.*"

"If I cannot, save yourself."

"There is nothing to save." He grabbed my hand, something he had never done. He nearly crushed my fingers. "*You* are everything."

"Gala?" said Beth. "Do you need help?"

"I found it!" I called loudly and stood, pulling free of Halen's grip and brandishing a golden ribbon that I spun from the straw.

"Pretty!" Alice exclaimed.

"Isn't it?" I twirled it above my head, pleased that it caught their eyes, relieved that they followed me out into the sun to see it gleam.

It took me a long time to understand what Halen had meant with those last words, what he'd really been saying.

I wish I had known.

I wish I had said, *I love you too*—though I don't know if I could have, not then. Maybe in a year. In ten. Maybe if he had found a way to say all those hundred other things first. Maybe if he had wept for what he had done to me. Maybe if I had.

Maybe then I wouldn't have had so many unspoken words to carry later. Words have power, but they have weight as well, and some of them are so terribly, terribly heavy.

I was nearly to the apple tree, where we were to have supper with Lyric, before I saw what she had done.

Spread out under the tree was a silvery blanket peppered with colorful cushions. A basket rested in the grass nearby, its lid open to reveal the sparkle of crystal, a gleam of golden plates, and parcels of food wrapped in white linen.

Clad in a gown of shimmering silver, Lyric sat reclining against the tree trunk, her legs extended and crossed at the ankles, her feet bare. Her auburn hair spilled, loose and luxurious, over her shoulders. She was humming a high, sweet tune and rolling an apple around in her hands. Laden with fruit, the tree's crooked branches bowed around her, draping low enough that only the man's boots were visible, hanging above the ground.

I froze, but the other girls continued on toward Lyric. Even this, they did not see. Because they preferred the illusion? Because their magic was weaker than mine? Or perhaps they simply did not know Lyric as I did and looked for nothing amiss.

"Hello, darlings," she trilled, smiling around at the others before her eyes lifted to mine. She looked at me as though curious.

Maybe I should have run right then and taken my chances. But there are some things you have to know, some answers more necessary than safety.

I walked on, my shoes crunching over the gravel, closer and closer to the tree. At first, I saw only a Trevarian uniform, the yellow and blue stained with blood, a nauseating mess of glistening entrails spilling from the split belly. But I knew the body's shape and size, the callused blacksmith's hands. Stepping under the tree's canopy, my eyes traveled up. The neck was wrong, stretched and twisted like that, and his face was swollen and purpled, but it was him.

Of course it was.

Lyric's sweet humming threaded through the light conversation of the girls. She watched as I collapsed onto the blanket, quaking with horror at the sight of Halen's suffering, of Lyric's casual comfort beside it.

Someone put a plate by my hand, the outstretched one that was keeping me upright. I might have remained in that state of shock for the whole evening, perhaps forever, if Lyric had not appeared at my side. I looked into her silvery eyes, eyes I would never understand. So intelligent and not without feeling. Warm even, where my own were cold.

"I told you," she hummed, "that he would pay for what he did to you."

They say that people burn with anger, that a temper is hot. Not for me. At Lyric's words, my heart froze in my chest, and my blood ran like an icy river.

Lyric held up an apple between us: it had one cheek that was red and the other was white. Where my own asymmetry made me ugly, the apple's made it beautiful. She lifted the apple to her mouth and bit into the red cheek, her fine, white teeth chomping out a greedy bite. Then, cheeks bulging with the apple's sweet flesh, she offered the bitten fruit to me.

I took it.

My eyes cut past Lyric to Halen's tortured body. Lyric had not even tried to pull me into her illusion; she wanted me to see what she had done to him. My fingers bit into the apple as fiercely as Lyric's teeth had done. I didn't give words to the spell. I gave it all the poisonous, icy rage of my heart.

For Halen's death.

For my father's.

For my mother's.

For Rose.

I poured the pain of all the screams I had never let out and all the tears I had never shed and all the terrible anger I had not even realized I carried into that apple, and my hand clenched and the fruit burst and Lyric let out a strangled cry.

Her eyes bulged. Blood ran from them, and she clutched at her throat, choking. Sickly green veins showed through her skin, threading down her face and neck. The apple's sticky pulp ran down my fingers and wrist into the sleeve of my moldy, ragged dress.

The girls started to scream and cry because, finally, *for once*, they could see.

Lyric collapsed and rolled onto her back, silvery eyes wide, face gruesome with poisoned veins. I climbed to my feet and stared down at her. Unlike with Halen, there was nothing I wanted to say to her.

I only wanted her to die.

Bile and blood and bubbly, greenish foam ran from her mouth as her lips parted—and she *laughed*. She laughed like she had never been happier in her life.

The girls were really screaming now. Pale-faced, dark-clothed figures were skittering toward us through the garden, hissing like cats.

"We have to go!" I shouted. I grabbed and shoved at the others until they stumbled into terrified compliance, and we fled through the orchard and flowerbeds toward the hidden gate. Demons converged on us, sweeping into our path, dozens of them, wild-eyed and tasting the air with their long, flickering tongues. Clawed fingers curled in the ground as they crouched to spring.

"*Get back, demons, and be gone!*" I commanded, swelling my words with power as I had that day in the woods when I dispelled the faerie path.

The demons twitched and howled at my words, but they did not disperse. They barely even slowed. The girls sobbed behind me.

Anger yet ran cold and fierce through my veins, and when a demon lunged for me, I seized it by the neck. It froze into a solid block of ice and toppled at my feet.

Someone screamed, and I wheeled to see Beth struggling in a demon's grasp. I dove for the creature and grappled with it, ice bursting from my hands to pierce its body.

Another grabbed my hair and yanked me off my feet. Its slimy tongue licked up my neck.

A roar that was somewhere between a stag's bellow and a man's shout ripped through the air. Shrieking, the demons skittered. The one with its claw digging into me loosened its grip enough that I could tear away.

The Hunter was storming toward me and the other girls, who were huddled and whimpering. His antlers reared from his head, and the light blazed between them like the sun. A pale sword appeared in his hand, and he hacked through a demon, cutting it in half.

All through the garden, roots burst from the ground and wrapped around the shrieking demons. I shouted at the girls and grabbed someone's hand—Sorsha's—and yanked. She stumbled after me, eyes wide with terror. Beth and Alice hurried after us as I led the way to the bramble of roses that hid the gate. Lyric's laugh, high and wild and full of mad joy, tumbled through the air.

Desperate to get to the gate, I ripped through the thorny canes, but they thickened and twined, seizing me and the others in a piercing, inescapable grip. Like the faerie path. Like the roots the Hunter had called up against the demons. Fae magic.

The branches tore at my skin as I wrenched around to see. Lyric, face streaked with dark, poisoned veins, eyes bleeding, greenish bile running down her chin, smiled with utter delight. The Hunter was on his knees before her, and her hand was wrapped around one of his antlers. He bellowed with rage. Shadows whipped around him, coiling tight, dimming the light that had blazed above him. When he threw back his head and bellowed again, he nearly yanked Lyric off her feet.

She let go of his antler, and the shadows thickened around him until he was swallowed completely. Then the shadows faded to nothing, and he was gone.

Lyric crossed the garden, crushing lilies as she went, perfuming the air with their destruction. "I knew," she said, smiling, "even when you were a child, I knew, my dear, that you would be the fairest of all."

Part 2.

Blood Red

9.

Silver and Cold

You were always my favorite.

When had Lyric spoken those words? That night in the garden? Sometime as we traveled to Trevar? Or on one of our many evenings in her lavish battlefield tent?

Somewhere along the way, I had lost track of time.

The golden quality of the light spilling through the gap in the tent flap and across my feet told me it was late summer. The afternoons had been peaking hot and humid, the evenings bringing cool relief. Fall was not far off. A month, I guessed, since Lyric had fastened the silver chain around my neck.

Thin and light, its tiny links so smooth I couldn't feel them, it was more a necklace than a chain—except that it had no clasp and was as strong as an iron lock. I'd tried every spell, every twist of magic I could think of, and pulling at it only made the metal cut into my throat and fingers.

If nothing else, I now understood the scope of Lyric's power. She ruled everything she set her hand to, from the teeming hordes on the battlefield to the finest strand of silver.

I had no idea what of the power was her own and what she had bargained for, or whether the difference mattered. I did know, however, that much of what Lyric gave her demonic allies in exchange for their help was not hers to give. Mostly, she gave the lives of others. Her horde hungered for mortality, feeding on the fear and bloodlust that only clashing armies can inspire. She had told me as much.

Lyric had led the horde—and a smattering of Cresilean soldiers and camp followers—into the hills of Trevar. I had traveled, collared, in her war wagon, or so she called the monstrosity. The spiderlike conveyance had a shiny black hull like a carapace. On its many-jointed, claw-tipped legs, it had scuttled along in the midst of Lyric's seething army, carrying me all the way to Trevar, even to the fields outside of the walled royal city of Kothe. Sometimes Lyric had ridden inside with me, humming and serene on the bench of red velvet. Sometimes she had not. As we traveled, I saw nothing of the other girls, nothing of the Hunter either.

After all those unsettling miles, with demons hissing and chittering and no longer pretending to be human outside the shell of the "wagon," the silver tent had been a relief. At first. But my hopes of escape had soon dimmed. The necklace tethered me inside the tent. I could walk the ten paces from one end to another, my steps cushioned by the overlapping rugs. I could sit in any chair, touch anything I liked. I could even look outside, if I wanted to gaze upon the blackened earth and the milling demons and the squatting, spiderlike forms.

Lyric said nothing of her plans for me, why she kept me alive, why she hadn't harmed me. Maybe she simply hadn't decided. She was busy, after all.

And there were those words: *You always were my favorite.* I think I hated her for that as much as for anything. Why should I be her favorite? What did that say about me?

I wasn't the only one who hated her. I wasn't the only one trapped by her.

I wasn't sure whether the Hunter had made a deal he now regretted, or whether his service had been unwilling from the start. Unlike mine, his bonds lay within. His mind was not his own, not fully, though he wasn't bewitched in the way my father had been. Lyric's control of the Hunter was more forceful, conquest rather than deception.

The first time he had emerged from the shadows within the tent, he had terrified me. His usually expressionless face had been contorted with rage—or maybe, I thought later, pain. I had scrambled away from him, stumbling over silk pillows, toppling chairs and candlesticks.

I knew better now.

I called to him now.

I worried when he didn't come.

As the light shifted from late afternoon into evening, lengthening the shadows, I whispered, "Are you there?"

My eyes sought movement; indeed all my senses were tuned to the tiny currents that would tell me I wasn't alone. Maybe that's why I called him. Maybe that's why he came. To not be alone.

In the corner, the shadows thickened then slid partway free of his crouched form. Usually, he stepped out, eerie and silent. Sometimes he stalked out in anger, raging wordlessly against something he had done—or, rather, that Lyric had done using his hands. Tonight, he remained crouched, caught in the spooling shadows. They licked over him, twining around his antlers, dimming the light that crowned him, trying to draw him back into their nothingness.

"Hunter," I said, moving up onto my knees.

His head lifted. His hazel eyes, which held all the browns and greens and golds of the autumn woods, were his own. The signs were subtle, but I was learning to see them: softness, awareness, depth. Sometimes he was more present than others. Right now, he was trembling. I had never seen him tremble.

I abhorred everything Lyric did, but there was something especially awful about her control of the Hunter. He was the wild woodland stag, bound and brutalized. He was the bright and ethereal Fae, dimmed and ruined. Yet I realized, as I watched him trembling in the shadows, that I had been thinking of him more as a thing than a person. He might not be human, but he *was* a person.

He felt anger. He felt pain. Surely he felt fear as well. He certainly suffered.

I inched closer to him.

He had touched me before: my neck and fingers, healing the cuts left by my frustrated tugging at the silver necklace. But I had never once reached out to him.

I did so now, my fingers seeking his where they were clamped on his bent knee. He jerked at the initial touch, but his grip slowly eased, his fingers relaxing under mine. Then, tentatively, his hand shifted, turning upright. I interlaced my fingers with his, and he let out a long, shuddering breath. What a strange pair we were: the ugly young witch and the beautiful, ageless Fae. Yet, we needed the same thing: to feel someone else's fingers for a moment. To not be alone.

I thought of Halen and how I had craved this simple thing from him without quite realizing it. How different things might have been between us if either had reached out a hand.

But it's hard to reach out to a stone. Easier by far to reach out to someone's pain. But had I not been in pain? Had Halen not? The difference, I think, was that neither of us had let it show. I was glad the Hunter let me see his. I was amazed to discover the doorway that it opened.

I think the Hunter was too. He gazed at our clasped hands like they were strange and beautiful, like he didn't know what to make of them.

He rarely spoke, and when he did it was only ever, *No*, like that night he had led me back to my room, so I was surprised when he said, "How?"

"How, what?" I asked when he'd fallen silent.

He frowned. Words were hard for him. Thoughts were hard for him.

I could see he was frustrated, so I said, "It's all right. You don't have to speak. Just ... don't go."

Desperation had crept into my voice. It was the kind of thing I didn't usually allow, but somehow—with the Hunter, in this moment—it felt safe to show that I was frightened.

His grip firmed, and his eyes became more present. The shadows slipped from him a little more, coiling around his feet.

"Snow," he said. He'd never said my name. I was surprised he knew it.

"Hunter." When his eyes dimmed, I felt a stab of guilt. For Lyric he was the Hunter; it wasn't his name. I didn't know his name, so I did what I should have done long ago. I asked him.

His lips parted then he shook his head like he couldn't tell me. Or maybe he couldn't remember.

"It's all right," I said again.

But it wasn't. Nothing that Lyric had done—to him or anyone—was all right.

The shadows took him back, as they always did, but it became a new normal for us when he appeared: one of us reaching out, the other accepting. Nothing was demanded, nothing taken—and only a small thing was given. But so much was received: comfort, acceptance, relief.

It confused me. It didn't fit with the way I'd learned to be in the world. And still I kept reaching out my hand.

Then one day he said, "Bregas." He gritted his teeth as though it hurt him to speak, but he ground out, "My name is Bregas."

Among the many luxuries of Lyric's tent was a black-and-silver checkered board with black and silver game pieces. It brought back old memories of Lyric, how she'd loved to play chess, how it was the one thing she and my father had had in common. He had usually won, but I wondered now: had she let him win, lulling him? Had she been studying his mind and methods?

The game pieces crouched on their squares like tiny winged demons and vicious, snapping horses and bristling crowns. The first time one of Lyric's silver pieces bit my finger, I nearly toppled from my chair in surprise. Lyric had laughed with delight, her mad, cruel eyes sparkling in the lamplight.

I had taken to freezing her pieces. It cut down on the cheating as well, for the silver figures had a habit of creeping into more advantageous squares when I wasn't watching.

One night, Lyric's rook, which I had already frozen, burst into flames when I picked it up. I dropped it with a yelp and cradled my burned fingers. Lyric smiled, but I stilled my own face—and kept it that way. Even when my knight stabbed his tiny obsidian sword through Lyric's palm, I kept it that way. Lyric's eyes widened. I met her gaze steadily across the board.

"I enjoyed it, you know," she said, idly smearing the blood around on her palm. "Watching you pretend all that time."

"Is that why you let me?"

Lyric's head tilted as she studied me. "There was much to learn in watching you. Do you know what pleased me best?"

"Thinking me a fool?" I said it coolly, as though I felt nothing at the words.

Lyric tsked. "No, my dear. What pleased me was how patient you were." Her smile brightened. "How you reminded me of myself! It takes a cold heart to dine with your enemy. And you weren't a fool—not until you let the dwarf escape. If I hadn't already marked you, I would have then, even though my Fae lordling took the blame for it. I didn't believe him, of course, but I pretended that I did. Pretending can be fun, can it not?"

My blood ran cold. "What did you do to him?"

"Nothing he didn't deserve."

I schooled my features, not wanting her to use him against me or to hurt him again on my account. The dwarf had spoken truly that night: *Someone will bear the blame. And, with it, the pain.* So easily I had accepted that without knowing what it would mean. So relieved I had been to think the whole thing forgotten. How had Bregas suffered for me that night?

Lyric continued to study me. "He's pretty—don't you think?"

I gave her nothing, but that was the thing with Lyric: she took when nothing was given. She heard when nothing was said.

<hr />

Lyric could change the dimensions of my invisible prison. For obvious reasons, such as me attempting to kill her, at night I could not move beyond my pallet.

Lyric could also take me with her, and one day she led me through the camp to the edge of the battlefield. The camp was a nightmare of pale, staring creatures and all too human screams. The smells of blood and waste and rot polluted the air as we walked along an impossibly long stretch of silver carpet. Tents dotted the grounds, some of cloth, others of shiny black slats that reminded me of the carapaces of the scuttling, spiderlike creatures squatting nearby. Gibbets stood here and there, some with bodies hanging. Bonfires raged and smoked.

And Lyric, all but glowing from within, strolled through it all as though through a sunny meadow.

The human soldiers and camp followers scattered among the demons disturbed me most of all. They lurked, hollow-cheeked and hungry-eyed. I could not tell whether they were bewitched by Lyric or prey to their own dark desires. Lyric might be the worst, but she was not alone in her wickedness.

One of the camp followers, an old woman hidden in a cloak of brownish red that reminded me of old blood, looked up from her cauldron as we walked the silver carpet. Gnarled hands clutched a long wood spoon, and a nose, hooked like an eagle's beak, protruded from the shadows of her hood. *Witch*, I thought, shivering.

Lyric and I reached a rocky overlook to see the battlefield, a stretch of charred earth before the blackened walls of Kothe. It would not be long before Lyric took the city. Dead men and dead horses dotted the field, and beasts with grotesque, leathery wings perched atop them, feeding.

"There's so much you don't know, niece." I flinched at Lyric's address. She didn't notice, or pretended not to. *Pretending can be fun, can it not?* I couldn't trust anything she showed me or anything she said. Even so, her next words gave me pause. "Aria never loved your father."

My heart skipped. It was the first time I'd heard my mother's name in seven years. She was "King Philip's first wife," if she was referred to at all.

"She didn't want to marry him, but she was woefully practical, your mother. One man had found our cottage. Others would follow. That is the way of things, for women.

Better to be the wife of a king, she said, than the wife of a woodsman. As if there were no other choices.

"But your father had darkness in his heart. A man who kills a swan is a man who destroys beauty. He destroyed your mother."

"That's a lie."

"It's not, my darling. It is what men do. Do you know what message the King of Trevar sent with his emissaries? A *marriage proposal.*"

I wanted to disbelieve her, but the revulsion in her face, in her voice ... I hadn't seen that in her since the moment before she plunged a dagger into my father's chest.

"Join me, niece," she said, her silvery eyes intent upon my face. "You are my blood. You are my daughter in heart. *Join me.* We will take this kingdom." Her fingers flicked casually toward the wasted plain before Kothe. "We will take a thousand kingdoms."

I recoiled. Of everything I might have expected from Lyric, this was the last.

"We are only safe," she said fiercely, "when we are in power." Her hand tightened into a fist—the very fist that had held the knife that night.

"You killed my father," I said.

She brushed that away. "To avenge my sister—your own mother."

"*You* killed my mother."

"*That's a lie!*" She wheeled on me and struck me hard across the face. I fell at her feet. "Your *father* killed her. He *suffocated* her. He would have suffocated you as well. You know *nothing!*"

"You killed my sister!"

Lyric rocked back as though I'd struck her. "Is that what you believe? Is that why you came to kill me, niece?"

I saw it then: the hurt in her eyes. It hurt her, actually *hurt her* that I wished her harm. Every time I thought I understood Lyric, she showed me that I didn't.

"You deserve to be punished," I said.

"That is your father speaking."

"He was a *good* man, and you killed him. Deny anything else you like, but that I *saw*."

She laughed bitterly. "Do you know why my mother was a swan by day? A *man* did that. *My own father* did that—because she did not love him the way he wanted. I told Aria—I *told* her that Philip would kill her—"

"But he didn't! My father didn't kill my mother! That isn't true!"

I was on my feet now, and angry. I didn't like what she was saying, the way she was twisting things. Her words remade my father into something else—my mother too.

And yet, my mother's own words came back to me: *A queen must be able to put her feelings aside.*

Had she meant that in relation to my father? Had she been unhappy with him? She had not seemed so to me, but I had been eleven years old when she died. What had I known, then? Had she resented her life in Orlas? Had she resented ... me?

Lyric regarded me sadly. "It is better to rule others than to be ruled, Snow. You are strong. You are cold. Join me. Let me show you what you can be."

For an instant, her words tempted me—gods help me, but they did. But it was the *words* that moved me, not her. Because I wanted to be what she described—safe, strong, powerful—but not in her way. I had only to seek what lay at the edge of my vision: the horror, the destruction. I did not want that. I did want to *be* that. I did not want to be *her*.

She sensed my withdrawal and said, a warning, a plea: "Rule, Snow—or be ruled."

I said nothing.

She offered a last temptation. "I would give him to you." The Hunter, she meant. But he was not hers to give. *No,* he'd said so many times. *No.*

It would do no good to say it to Lyric, but I said it inside: *No.* I would rather die. I would rather fight her and lose and die. Her way of ruling was a travesty, a perversion, and I would have none of it, not even to save my life.

A tear slipped down Lyric's cheek, then she looked away from me, out across the charred earth and the feasting of her demonic beasts. "This isn't what I wanted," she said. "But the things life makes us do …"

She shook her head, sorrowing.

10.

Friend or Foe?

She'll kill you eventually."

At my words, Sorsha paused, her hand hovering over the lid of Lyric's trunk. I had been so relieved the first time I'd spotted her trailing Lyric through the camp—until I'd realized that the position I had refused had been offered to her. And she had taken it.

Sorsha opened the trunk and knelt before it. "You're wrong."

"You know I'm not."

A curtain of mousy hair swept down to hide her face as she ducked her head. "Don't tell me what I know."

"Where are the others? Alice and Beth—where are they?"

"You should be more concerned about yourself," Sorsha mumbled.

"Because she's going to kill me? You think I don't know that? She will kill all of us. Me, you, Beth and Alice if they're not already dead. Look around you. Nothing good can come of serving her."

"And what good can come of refusing?"

When I didn't have a ready answer, Sorsha reached into the trunk. The air thickened with pressure around her, as though the space was rearranging itself.

My breath caught when she pulled out the spell book. I'd been through that trunk a dozen times. I'd hunted every nook and cranny of this tent.

Sorsha tucked her curtain of hair behind her ear, and her slumped shoulders drew back. "She trusts *me*."

My mind raced with possibilities, and I found myself inching toward her. "*Use it.* Sorsha—find a way, a spell, to free me, and we'll escape together. The others too." When her expression darkened, I halted. "They're dead. Aren't they?"

Sorsha's hands started shaking, and she hugged the book to her chest. "I know she's ... But she's ... She *sees* me. I can ... *be* something."

"You won't like what you become."

She stiffened, but her head didn't drop, that curtain of hair didn't fall. Her chin jutted out and she climbed to her feet still clutching the book. "You don't know what I would like. And how could you understand? You, a king's daughter."

"She *killed my father.*"

"And I killed mine."

"It was an accident," I said, recalling Sorsha's story of her father falling on his plow.

"No," she replied with new firmness. "It wasn't an accident. Her Majesty understands that—that it's not wrong to punish bad people, that they deserve what happens to them."

As Sorsha stalked across the tent, I wondered if I could seize the book from her. Even if I did, I couldn't hope to make use of it in time. With the silver chain around my neck, I was bound to this tent.

I followed Sorsha to the tent flap, watched as she made her way across the blackened ground, through the horde of demons that didn't dare touch Lyric's treasure. Lyric herself was a silver figure in the distance. I couldn't see her face, but I could imagine her smile.

I would try again. I didn't believe Sorsha about punishing her father. That was Lyric, twisting Sorsha's story as she had tried to twist my mother's. Magic could be unruly, tied to emotion. Young witches, unguided, could do harm without intending it. If I had another chance to speak to Sorsha, I would try to persuade her.

But to do what? To risk her life? To throw away the protection she currently had? If demons and the stink of death did not set her against Lyric, what would? Hope, maybe … but I had none to offer her.

Discouraged, I was about to duck back inside the tent when I spotted a small, hunched figure in a cloak of brownish red the color of old blood. It was the crone I'd seen that day when Lyric had led me through the camp to the battlefield. The witch.

Of her eyes I could see nothing, but the hooked nose protruding from the hood of her cloak said she was looking my way. She'd moved closer to Lyric's tent and had brought her cauldron with her. As before, she was stirring it, her hands like gnarled old roots clutching the wooden spoon.

Shuddering, I withdrew into the tent.

That night, the table where Lyric and I ate and sometimes played chess draped itself with a white tablecloth. Candles shimmered into existence. Two golden plates appeared, each covered with a silver cloche, along with platters of roasted meats and vegetables, a basket of fresh rolls, and tureens of creamy soup. Wine poured itself from a green bottle into two crystal glasses. We always ate well, but this went beyond the usual offerings. It chilled me to think that Lyric had something to celebrate.

In the early days, I had refused to eat, but I was too practical for such protests. Weakening myself served no one but Lyric, and if she wished to kill me—with poison or steel or magic—there was little I could do about it.

I understood now that she had kept me alive in the beginning in the hopes of persuading me to join her cause. What was her purpose now that I had refused? Did she still hope to convince me? Had she paraded Sorsha and the spell book before me today to spark jealousy?

All she was doing was making me hate her more.

I had not seen Bregas since the day she'd offered him to me like a prize. Had she harmed him? Killed him? Obliterated the last vestiges of his mind?

She must have been aware of our time together, or else she would not have known he might tempt me. She must have allowed it so she could use him as a lure. A terrible thought had occurred to me since then: that Bregas had perhaps been acting on her orders, pretending all along. I didn't want to believe that, but I couldn't discount the possibility.

Lyric ducked into the tent. As her eyes traveled the length of my body, she sighed. "My dear, you really must take more care with your appearance."

I'd been wearing the same blue dress for weeks, months maybe. Filthy and stinking, ragged at the hems and torn at one elbow, it was disgusting. I wanted it to be disgusting because I wanted it to be the truth. Every time Lyric laid an illusion over it, I stripped it away.

She waved a hand, and the dress transformed: the silk gleaming in the candlelight, the tears all gone, the reek dissipating. Lyric nodded. "Much better. This is a special night. I can't have you in rags."

I would restore its ruin later. Right now, I had other concerns.

"What are we celebrating?" Had Kothe fallen? Was King Stefan's head on a pike somewhere?

"Enjoying," Lyric corrected, flowing into her seat like liquid silver. "Savoring."

She did love her word games, but I wasn't in the mood for them tonight. Not that I ever was. I thumped into the chair across from her. "What will you do with Sorsha?"

"Did you enjoy her visit? It's good to spend time with girls your own age."

"Were you testing her by having her retrieve the book—or teasing me?"

I didn't expect an answer, didn't even want one. But I did not like silence with Lyric. She would start humming. It drove me nearly mad when she did that.

Sometimes I feared she would take words from me as she had from Bregas, but I think she enjoyed our conversations like she enjoyed our games of chess.

Lyric drummed her fingers on the silver cloche covering her plate. "Do you know why I spoil the girls?"

The question startled me into exposing my interest. I had often wondered that. "Why?"

Lyric smiled like she'd just moved one of her pawns into a prime position. "Young women like you—and like Sorsha even—are rare. Most are simple little creatures, prone to fancies and given to fears." She shrugged an elegant shoulder. "I prefer to cultivate the former."

I frowned, not following. "You were teaching them magic."

"Enriching them with it, yes. The heart, you see, is everything. The *center* of magic. The *essence* of it. I gave them delight. I let their magic blossom from pleasure. The girls could have lived out their lives in those blissful dreams." Giving me a reproachful look, she said, "You took that from them, my dear."

Lyric uncovered her plate and set the silver cloche aside. A piece of dark, smooth meat the size of a fist lay in the middle of the golden plate. A faint glow pulsed from it. Lyric picked up her knife and fork and sliced into it. Blood oozed out to puddle on the plate. The meat was raw.

The meat was not meat, not exactly.

Lyric lifted the glowing slice to her mouth, her teeth pulling at the dense bite, blood staining her lips bright red. Her eyelids fluttered with pleasure as she chewed.

"There is a different flavor," she said after swallowing, "to fear."

I stared. As ice crept over my skin, I stared and stared and stared.

"But fear can blossom like love, sometimes more intensely." Lyric cut into the heart again and shrugged delicately. "Every witch is different."

Lyric had not been feeding the girls to her demon allies. She had been eating them herself. Their hearts at least. She was eating their magic.

That was why she had been practically glowing that day in Orlas after Vivianne had disappeared. That was why she was starting to glow now.

That was why she had so much power.

Lyric took another bite, watching the understanding that must have been growing in my eyes. She smiled, pleased, and said as she had once before, "What big eyes you have, my love."

Ice raced out from my fingertips where they gripped the edge of the table. It ghosted white and sheer across the feast, freezing the food, snuffing the candles, spreading out all around me until everything in the tent—the bed, the chairs, the canvas walls—glittered with ice.

The candles sparked back to life between me and Lyric. Her lips were tinged blue, but still she smiled and exhaled a cloudy plume into the cold air.

"Oh, my dear," she marveled and cut into the heart again, her fingers pale with cold, ice crusting her silver sleeves and frosting the curling tips of her auburn hair. Only the heart had not frozen. Too rich, perhaps, in magic, still pulsing out its glow. The seeping blood steamed against the golden plate, which glittered with a lace of frost.

Lyric met my eyes as she lifted another bite to her lips, not reacting even when icicles burst from the ground all around her. One skimmed her cheek, drawing a thin line of blood. Her lips curved into a wicked smile as she dared me to try again.

I lunged across the table for her, but I was yanked back by the neck, pain slicing my throat. I fell hard to the icy ground but scrambled up. Jagged blades of ice burst from my hands. I would kill her. Here and now, I would kill her if it was the last thing I did.

The chain seized tight around my neck, cutting my skin, choking me. I thrust my hands her way, and ice sliced the air between us. I would make it slice right through her.

But the chain tightened and tightened until I couldn't breathe and couldn't feel anything but its bite. Blackness crowded in at the edges of my vision, like the shadows creeping across the mirror in Lyric's room.

Snoooooowwwwhiiiite.

"She is mine!" Lyric shouted. "Do you hear me, Kraxikel? Stay *back*! She is *mine*!"

The blackness closed, and I knew no more.

———

I woke shivering on my pallet to the sound of dripping. Sunlight speared in through the tent's slightly open flap, sparkling over the melting ice, glittering within the droplets of water that wept from the icicles, lighting up clouds of fog that moved lazily through the tent.

I was soaked and cold.

I was alive.

My fingers explored my tender throat and found a crust of dried blood—and the chain, of course. My fingers curled around it as cold anger seized my heart. If I pulled hard enough—

"I wouldn't do that."

The unfamiliar voice creaked from outside the tent flap. I scrambled up.

"Unless you want to die?" A hooked nose speared through the gap and a gnarled hand curled around the cloth. The crone in the brownish red cloak hobbled into the tent, fog swirling around her.

"Who are you, witch?" I tried to ready myself to fight or flee, but I was shaking with cold, my teeth clacking with it.

She cackled like I'd made a delightful joke then sobered to say, "There's not much time."

"Time for what?"

The crone hobbled around the tent, flipping open boxes and dumping out jewels and trinkets, ignoring them all. She went to Lyric's trunk and flung it open with surprising strength for such a shriveled old woman. "Escape," she said, pawing through the trunk with gnarled hands that thrummed with magic.

"Escape?"

Shouts outside made my head whip around. I hurried to the tent flap and peered out to see fog as thick as cream seeping through the camp. Dark, obscured shapes skittered through it, hissing and chittering. Of Lyric, I could see nothing.

The crone appeared at my elbow, startling me. A gnarled hand reached out, bony fingers beckoning, whispers slipping from beneath her shadowed hood. I shuddered as something slid around my neck—no, slid free of it.

My hand jumped to my throat as the silver chain slithered through the air like a thin snake and coiled within the old witch's hand. She poured the chain into a small leather pouch and whispered it shut before tucking it inside her cloak.

"What do you want with that thing?" I demanded.

"You would waste it?"

"I would destroy it if I could."

"Then you're a fool." She leaned past me to look out at the war camp, croaked, "Follow me," then slipped outside.

I hesitated only a moment. Even if she meant me harm, it could not be worse than Lyric. I hurried after her.

A demon hissed and snatched at me through the fog. With a yelp, I sent a spear of ice through its eye.

"Hurry!" the crone screeched over her shoulder.

From somewhere in the miasma came the eerie bellow of a stag.

"Wait!" I called to the crone. "Bregas! I must—"

The witch's gnarled hand seized on mine like a talon and she yanked me along. "Leave him!"

The bellow sounded again, closer, and Lyric's voice shouted from somewhere. "Hunter! Do not let them escape!"

I stumbled as the crone hauled me along. There was no hope of escaping the camp. There was no way out.

Ahead of us, a bulbous dark shape appeared in the fog. The witch's cauldron. It bulged, growing to unnatural size.

Light bled over my shoulder, diffused by the haze but unmistakable. I looked back as Bregas stalked my way, his antlers piercing the fog, the shadows lashing around him.

The cauldron rang like a bell as the crone leaped inside. As I dove in after her, pain lashed across my scalp.

The last thing I saw before the cauldron whipped into a spin was Bregas's empty eyes and the long ebony strands of my hair dangling from his fist.

Somewhere in the fog, Lyric howled with rage.

11.

The Witch in the Wood

As the spinning cauldron slowed by degrees, the colors whirling around me were no longer the black and gray of the war camp but rather green and brown. The cauldron eased to a stop. Through the fog coiling up from the cauldron's belly, I could see that we were surrounded by trees. Blue sky showed through the branches. Wherever we were, it was far from the haze of the battlefield.

The witch clambered out of the cauldron, one sharp elbow digging into my ribs, the wooden heel of her boot crushing my hand. As nausea crested like a wave inside me, I closed my eyes. That only made it worse, so I clutched the rim of the cauldron and stared out at the trees, willing my stomach to settle.

"Blood and bones!" spat the crone. "Fire and fog! Curse it all!"

Magic crackled from her gnarled fingers, which she flicked toward the ground. There was a pop and hiss like water splattering in a hot pan.

As the cauldron began to contract around me, I scrambled out with a yelp. The cauldron shrank to the size of a soup pot and teetered its way to stillness, fog still coiling from its mouth.

The crone aimed a long, gnarled finger at me. "Mark my words: that thing will be after us!"

I swatted at her wrist. I did not appreciate being pointed at like that, especially by a finger that had been crackling out such temperamental magic mere moments ago. She grabbed a handful of my sodden hair, examining the broken ends.

"Fire and flood!" she cursed, tossing my hair away. It splatted against my wet back.

The Hunter. She meant the Hunter would be after us, that he would use my hair to track me.

"He's not a 'thing,'" I said, pushing to my feet and rubbing my arms for warmth. "His name is Bregas—"

"Bah!" She flapped a bony hand then snatched up the cauldron, spitting into its belly. The last of the fog vanished. "What you call him won't matter when he's cutting out your heart for that vile hag!"

The words screeched out from the crone's dark hood with a certain irony, though in truth I knew nothing of her face beyond the hooked beak of her protruding nose.

"Show me your face."

"Why? What do you think a face means?"

Half of mine was ruined, so to me? A face meant a lot. But it was the eyes that truly spoke, and I needed to see hers.

At my insistent look, the crone shook her head in annoyance but flung back her hood, exposing a weathered old face. Not old—ancient. The woman's white hair was coiled at her nape in a long braid, and a yellow kerchief was tied over it. Deep lines gouged the skin framing her mouth, pulling it into a frown, and her neck was a loose wattle. Crow's feet clawed out from her eyes, but the eyes themselves ...

They were brilliant sapphires, too bright for her old face. Chills tightened my skin at the summer sky color.

"Happy?" she croaked, those sapphire eyes challenging me.

"Who are you?"

"Who are *you*?" she shot back.

"You must know who I am. Why else would you have freed me?"

She leered at me. "Maybe for your magic. Maybe I'll bake you into a pie and eat you myself. Or chain you to a spinning wheel until you've spun a thousand sheaves of straw into gold. Will you run?"

I shuddered. All she described—that was what old women of the woods did, according to the storytellers. "Would it do me any good to run, witch?" If she was powerful enough to circumvent Lyric's magic, she was powerful enough to stop me.

The crone shifted her cauldron, almost a nervous gesture, and said in annoyance, "Oh, just come along."

"I'll go my own way," I hedged, half testing whether she would force me, half out of a sense of fairness. She didn't owe me her protection. "If the Hunter is after me, I should get as far away from you as possible."

"He'll kill you."

Would he? I'd seen his eyes, empty and terrible. I knew he was bound to Lyric's will. And yet ... he'd stopped at the rim of the cauldron. Had I been beyond his reach—or had he chosen not to reach at all?

That didn't mean I was safe from him.

"Why should you care?" I demanded.

The crone snorted and tugged her hood back up. "You cost me my chance to kill the queen. At the least, you owe me information."

"If you were there to kill Lyric, why didn't you?"

"And let you die?" The gnarled hand clenched on the cauldron's round belly.

"Why not? What could my life possibly be worth to you?"

"Bah! Just come along!"

I flung up my hands with an exasperation that made me feel like I was ten years old. I could not force answers from her, nor be sure of her intentions, but she had liberated me, and in doing so had likely saved my life. Besides, I had no better options.

The witch's cottage lay nearby. It was made from the woods: river stone and mud mortar, coarse reeds for thatch, its porch and doors and shutters of roughhewn oak and ash. Chickens strutted and scratched in the yard, and one of the goats was on the roof.

I had no business feeling at ease, but the sight did comfort me—and gave me an unexpected pang of homesickness. I hoped someone had taken Prickle in. I hoped they were milking her and not eating her. When you leave things behind, their fate is no longer yours to control.

"Get down!" the old woman admonished, flapping a gnarled hand. When the goat argued in bleating tones, she threatened, "If you eat the thatch again, I'll mend the cottage with your skin!"

After a final bleat, the goat jumped down onto the woodpile and into its rickety pen.

Muttering, the witch led me to her gate. She whispered over the latch before opening it then stepped through onto a path of flat blue stones.

I hesitated. "What spell lies on this gate?"

"If you mean me no harm, you have nothing to fear. The gate will know what lies in your heart, and if you carry murder or thievery there, you will find yourself stepping into a place you did not expect—and will not enjoy."

Well ... that seemed entirely reasonable to me. I envied her such a spell and wondered if she would teach it to me. As I passed through the gate, I felt a question wash over me but nothing more.

The chickens fled, clucking, as the crone and I trod the path of blue stones and went up the creaking porch steps to the door. I wondered if we would pass through another spell, but I felt only a brush of welcome and safety.

The cottage was a single room with a loft. It was larger than it looked from the outside, and the floor was neatly swept. Bunches of dried herbs hung from the rafters under the loft. The sight of a spinning wheel gave me pause after her jest, but a rolag of ordinary wool dressed the distaff.

Not everything was so homey. The bottles and jars crowding her shelves held powders and liquids that did not look culinary. Strings of bone hung like wind chimes, and a spider web in one high corner felt unnervingly watchful. Candles of every color cluttered the many surfaces.

The old woman took off her cloak and hung it on a peg by the door, exposing a shapeless dress of brown wool. She walked over to a shelf, where a squeaking mouse was racing past the jars. When she extended a gnarled hand, the mouse skittered across her palm and up her arm, vanishing into the folds of her loose dress.

Unsure what to do with myself, I stood there like a fool and watched the old woman hobble around her cottage. She set the cauldron by the hearth then spoke a word into the banked coals. A fire crackled to life. With her back to me, she whispered into her shoulder then chuckled softly.

The old woman stumped off to the space under the loft, where a bed was covered in a worn but tidy quilt. A trunk rested at the foot of the bed. Rummaging inside, she hauled out a frock of heavy blue wool and an armful of other items. She tossed them onto the bed then returned to the main room and grabbed a linen towel from a cupboard.

She thrust the towel in my direction. When I didn't move to take it, she gave it an impatient shake. "For your hair."

"Thank you."

"You can change over there." She jerked her chin toward the bed, where she had left the clothes. "There's a curtain if you're shy."

"What is your name?" I asked my rough-mannered hostess.

Giving me a sly look from under the ridge of her brow, she answered, "Witch is fine."

My face heated. I *had* been calling her that. "Surely you have a name?"

"What's wrong with witch?"

"It's not a name."

"I also respond to 'old woman' and 'you there.' Take your pick."

I gave up. "I'd like to wash myself first." I hadn't bathed in weeks. Even my desperation for clean, dry clothes could not override my disgust at the smell and feel of my skin.

"There's a wash barrel by the goat pen." With that, she hobbled over to a shelf and snatched up a basket. Then, muttering toward her shoulder at, I assumed, the mouse, she stumped her way to the door and left.

I went out to the goat pen and found a half barrel of tepid water. A scrubbing cloth draped the rim, and a cake of soap sat on a fence post. After a glance around that confirmed I was alone—except for the goat eyeing me from within her shelter—I stripped out of the sodden gown I'd been wearing for weeks. Several seams ripped as I extracted myself from the half-rotted garment. Shivering, I dropped it on the ground and thought longingly of burning it.

Crouching in the barrel, I splashed and scrubbed until my skin was raw then stepped out, dripping, so I could dunk my head and give my hair a scrub. It would be a horrid tangle, but it would be *clean*. Until I'd spent months wearing Lyric's moldy gowns, I had not realized how much I hated being dirty.

After squeezing water from my hair, I reached for the towel—which was not where I'd left it. It was a foot farther away. Inside the goat pen. Dangling from the goat's mouth.

I reached through the rails and snagged the end, yanking it away from the troublesome creature who was giving me the eeriest sense of familiarity.

She protested with a bleat that was just too … Prickle-like. And her tawny and black coloring echoed uncannily, not to mention the striped markings down her nose. Then two summer-grown kids came cavorting out from behind the shelter. One had a black ear. None of the animals' colors or patterns were unusual, but …

"Prickle?" I said, feeling absurd. When I reached out a hand, she nipped my fingers. "Ouch! You little vixen!"

The kid with the black ear made her head-bobbing way to me. I hadn't named Prickle's kids because I hadn't known whether Halen and I would keep them. Names mattered, whatever the witch might say. A name changed a person; it made them into someone.

The black-eared kid head-butted my elbow where it was resting on the fence. I shivered at the strangeness—and the chill. Wrapping the towel around myself, I left the ruined gown and the oddly familiar goats and returned to the cottage.

The witch didn't come back all day.

Dressed in the simple but clean garments she'd left for me, I busied myself with familiar chores in an unfamiliar place. I collected eggs and cleaned the chicken coop, swept the cottage even though it didn't need it. I weeded a little, but many of the witch's plants were unknown to me and I didn't want to stick my hands where they didn't belong.

As afternoon dimmed to evening, I rummaged around her larder to find onions, garlic, and carrots. A crock held butter, and I found some salt. It was the start of a meal at least, and I was starving. I had helped myself to some bread earlier in the day when my stomach ached so much from hunger that I felt sick. It rubbed me wrong to be eating someone else's food without invitation, but the witch's gruff hospitality had not extended to that.

When she returned, grunting at my cooking efforts, she busied herself with the herbs she'd harvested. Then she hobbled around doing things only she knew the purpose of, so I ignored her and stirred the thin soup. She came over and threw in a handful of herbs.

"You're a terrible cook," she complained.

"I didn't want to help myself to more than the simplest things. You left no instructions."

She sniffed through her hooked beak of a nose and hobbled off. She was uncomfortable with me. It was strange to realize that, given her power and position over me. I was a beggar in her house, wholly dependent on her mercy.

"Here," she grumbled, returning to me with a steaming mug.

When I accepted it, she elbowed me out of the way and took command of the soup.

I went to the kitchen, looking for something to do with myself as I sipped the sweet brew. "What is this?" I asked, wondering whether honey had been used to mask something sinister.

"Tea."

It was obviously tea. "Of *what?*"

"It's restorative," was all the answer I got.

She spoke truly. After a few sips, the last of my chill vanished. I hadn't even been aware of it, so accustomed had I grown to being cold. But suddenly I was warm to the fingertips. I sighed in relief. Stirring the soup, the crone glanced over her hunched shoulder at me.

"Thank you," I said, aware of the new ease in my voice. Maybe I had been a little prickly before. Which reminded me. "Your goats are ... interesting."

The witch did not acknowledge my thanks, her attention having returned to the pot. That was another thing I wanted to know about. The soup pot was the cauldron we had traveled in. I hadn't been sure whether to use it for the soup, but there had been no other pot to use, and the witch had left it by the hearth. After staring into it, sniffing it, and pressing an ear to it, I'd found nothing but cast iron, so I'd hooked it onto the fireplace chain, hoping wildly that I wasn't about to turn onions into eyeballs or something equally awful.

The witch sniffed at my comment on the goats. "Terrible, rude creatures."

"Have you had them a while?"

"The awful beasts turned up entirely uninvited a month or so ago. I've had no end of trouble, and I can't imagine what the bear is going to do."

"The *bear*?"

"He spends the winter here sometimes."

Putting that bizarre statement aside for the moment, I focused on the goats. "A month ago, you say?"

"Why?"

"You don't know where they came from?"

"If I did, I'd send them straight back."

Not ready to think more on that troubling revelation, I moved to my other topic. "That cauldron," I said, letting the words hang, hoping she would offer something. She didn't, so I went on, "It's powerful."

"It is."

"I didn't see anything else to cook in." She chuckled at my implied question of, *Was it* safe *to cook in?* I wasn't going to eat that soup until I was sure.

"There is power," she said, "in being able to serve many purposes."

When I complained, "You're as cryptic as Lyric," the witch snarled over her shoulder. I straightened, remembering that she was dangerous.

"It's just a pot," she snapped.

"I didn't mean to insult you."

She ignored me.

After adding mushrooms and greens to the soup, she left it steaming enticingly over the fire and hobbled into the larder. She emerged with a wheel of cheese and the remainder of the loaf I had cut into. I resisted the urge to apologize, and she said nothing of it.

We ate at her table, and it was the first meal I'd had since leaving Thistledown that had not appeared magically before me. Nothing had ever tasted better. After the first tantalizing bites upon my arrival at the castle, the fine flavors had sat poorly with me. I had resented all those little luxuries, the duplicity of them. The witch's simple fare suited me better.

She sniffed throughout the meal, disapproving of me—or so I assumed. She would look at me only from beneath the jutting ridge of her brow. At least that prominent bone with is thin white eyebrows hid her intensely blue eyes. Those eyes disturbed me. Deeply.

After, when I asked where I could wash the bowls, she waved an impatient hand toward the hearth. *Go sit there and stop bothering me*, the gesture said.

Fine.

I went to sit on the sheepskin rug. She had only one chair, a big rocker with a worn cushion on the seat, and I wasn't going to take her spot. While the witch clattered around in the kitchen, I watched the flames. The heat warmed the unblemished side of my face. The other side felt dead, as always.

At home—rather, in Thistledown—I had often made myself sit before the crackling hearth. I hated the fire ... but I hated fear more. Fear had made me weep and run from my father's death. It had made me leave my sister behind. It had meant seven years of hiding.

Fear had meant I'd failed to strike out at Lyric—until Halen was hanging, disemboweled, from a tree.

Fear had meant I'd watched Lyric eat someone's heart.

I squeezed my eyes shut. Curse the witch for taking away my busyness, for making me sit here and think. When she hobbled over and thrust a pottery cup at me, I took it automatically. She dropped into her chair, a gnarled hand curled around her own cup. I sipped with caution. Honey-sweet again, but not tea. Mead.

I didn't much care for sweets. Rose had been the one who'd begged for them. I slashed that thought away and sipped the mead. If nothing else, it gave me something to do.

"Why were you in ... that woman's camp?"

My hand jerked in surprise at the question, sloshing mead over the rim. Transferring the cup to my other hand, I licked the sticky spill from my thumb. After avoiding me all day, now she wanted to leap straight into things?

"That's a long story," I hedged.

The old woman set her chair to rocking. *I have all night*, the gesture said.

It wasn't a long story actually, not the way I told it. Or it wouldn't have been long if she hadn't interrupted me at every turn wanting to know *why* I did this or that.

"I don't know," I snapped at one point, exasperated.

"You didn't have a reason for trying to intervene when that woman"—that was how she always referred to Lyric—"took the girl away?" She was referring to the ball and Vivianne being "chosen."

"It was obviously not for something good."

"Aren't you pure?" the witch sneered. "Always so perfect."

I glared at her. She didn't know me. She didn't know that I *had* to stop Lyric, that I *had* to kill her. I had failed my family, and I had to avenge them. That lay at the heart of my decisions. I tried to tell myself it was justice, that it was to liberate the kingdom. It wasn't that I *didn't* care about that, but ... it was Lyric's too-sweet smile that haunted me, her trilling laugh. It was the way she twisted everything around to make herself into some kind of hero.

It was the empty place inside me where everything I loved had been ripped away. It was the cold, hard anger that echoed in that space.

"You don't know me," I said, my voice soft after these revelations had shown me to myself, small and awful.

"What happened next?" the witch asked, slightly less gruff.

After I'd reached the end of the story, the old woman gazed thoughtfully into the fire. The light played over her weathered face, shadowing the crevices of age and glaring along the hooked beak of her nose.

Her fingertips drummed on the arms of her rocking chair. Her yellowed nails were clogged with dirt from her foraging. She had stopped rocking, her earth-toughened feet going still.

Finally, she asked, "Did you ever see Kraxikel outside a mirror?"

"No."

"And you made no bargain with him?"

"Of course not."

"Bargains with demons are binding." Her tone held a warning. Why? Did she think me a liar?

"What bargain do think Lyric has struck with him?" I asked.

The old woman replied grimly, "One that won't serve her, not in the end. Bargains with demons are not only binding but unclear—at least to the human fool who makes them. Whatever their bargain, it serves him. Awful that woman might be, but Kraxikel ..." She trailed off, and I did not like the haunted look in her eyes.

"You said you were in the war camp to kill Lyric. Why? How does her death serve you? What's your interest in all of this?"

The witch sniffed. "That is not your business."

"I disagree."

"This is my house," she said petulantly. "You don't get to make demands, not here."

I gritted my teeth, repressing the urge to argue. It *was* her house, and she was dangerous, but it was hard not to bicker with her.

When I didn't reply, the witch pushed herself up from her chair with a grunt. As she stumped off toward the curtained alcove, she said gruffly, "There's a cot in the loft," and whipped the curtain shut.

I don't know what made me creep across the cottage floor late in the night when the moon was high. I don't know what made me pull back that curtain.

Maybe I knew the truth, deep down.

Maybe I'd known from the moment she threw back her hood after we'd stepped from the cauldron into the woods, when I saw those sapphire eyes.

There are some things, though, that a person isn't ready for, that have to sit in the back of the mind for a time and inch forward. Maybe that was what was happening, why I was acting without really thinking. The mind is strange, how it hides things from us, how we hide things from ourselves.

Moonlight cut across the bed at her waist. Her hand lay atop the covers. The skin was smooth and pale, the bones fine and perfect.

Her head rested in the deeper shadows, but I could make out a long spill of thick hair. I could not see the color, but it wasn't the witch's white braid, that was for certain.

Maybe she was under an enchantment, as my grandmother had been, a swan by day and a woman by night. Maybe that hand would age with the sun, the hair thin and whiten.

Or maybe she had lied to me.

12.

Truth and Trouble

Dawn bled the darkness away, revealing the truth by such slow increments that I barely noticed it happening. I felt no shock, only growing certainty. And hurt.

As light returned more color to her hair, the shadowy gray gave way to a red that deepened and brightened. Like a ruby. Like a rose. Morning pushed the shadows away from her face, revealing her smooth young neck and fine jaw, her pink lips and delicate nose.

She had always been beautiful. Seven years had only refined that.

She drew the deeper breaths of a sleeper waking then her sapphire eyes opened, locking on me.

"You lied to me." My voice was barely a whisper.

For a moment, she looked like a cornered animal, frightened and desperate, then her eyes hardened. She sat up roughly and looked away. "What did you expect?"

"Not a lie. Not from you."

Her eyes jumped back to me. She scowled. "Blood and bones, you're so *pure*."

"Why did you lie to me, Rose?"

I had never thought to see her again, so I had never imagined our reunion. If I had, I wouldn't have imagined this: me, cold; her, hostile.

"I don't use that name anymore."

"Why did you lie to me?"

Her pretty pink lips curled. "I suppose you never lie?"

"I wouldn't lie to you."

With a curse, she flung the covers aside and launched herself from the bed, ripping the curtain aside and stalking out into the cottage, her shift flapping around her slim calves.

"Rose—"

She wheeled on me. "My *name* is Blood Red."

At my recoil, she gave a bitter laugh. Shaking her head, she stalked over to where she'd left her boots, smashed her feet into them, and yanked her cloak off its hook—the cloak whose color had reminded me of an old bloodstain. I heard a rip, but she didn't pause, only whirled the cloak around her shoulders.

"Where are you going?"

"Out," she snapped.

"Out?"

"*Away.*"

"Away?"

"From *you*," she clarified nastily and wrenched open the door. She sailed out then snapped the door shut behind her.

I stared at the door, its slam echoing in my ears, her words echoing too. My heart was racing as though I'd been running.

When I heard the gate shriek on its hinges, I hurried out of the cottage after her, racing down the path of blue stones. "Wait!"

She didn't. I ran after her, roots and stones tearing at my bare feet, branches catching at the hem of the blue woolen dress I wore. Her dress. My sister's.

With me smashing through the undergrowth like a clumsy boar, she must have heard me coming, but she didn't respond until I grabbed at her. "Rose—"

She spun out of my grasp, out of my path. Surging past her, unable to catch my balance, I crashed to my hands and knees. I twisted to face her as she aimed a finger at me, not the gnarled finger of the old crone but the fine finger of a seventeen-year-old girl. There was nothing fine or girlish in her voice, however.

"You will not call me that. *Rose* is dead. I am *Blood Red*."

I could do nothing but stare at her. I hated the name. I hated the way she was looking at me with such contempt. I hated that she was a stranger to me.

With too many questions to focus on a specific one, I only managed a vague and desperate, "Why?"

"You may not have changed, sister, but I have."

At that, anger spilled through me, cooling my blood, slowing my heart. I climbed stiffly to my feet. "Do I look unchanged to you?"

Her gaze was unwavering. Relentless. Unmoved. Who was this fierce stranger?

"Why did you lie to me?" That was the knife in my heart, the reason I couldn't quite breathe. She had known who I was. Even before saving me, she had known. She had brought me here and let me tell my story, knowing all the while. She had let me fear her.

"Bah!" she exclaimed, sounding like the withered crone she had shown to me, and turned away. Her gorgeous red hair spilled down her back, so much like Lyric's but brighter and richer and far more beautiful.

"You were in the war camp to kill her," I said. Her shoulders were heaving. Her back was still to me. "But you saved me instead."

My sister crossed her arms, not responding.

"Red." That was as far as I could go with her name.

She turned slowly, her brilliant sapphire eyes burning with a heated anger so different from my own terrible coldness. I envied her. And feared her still. Where had she learned such magic? No simple illusion had transformed into that withered crone; I would have seen through it. She had wielded some deeper magic. And the cauldron. The gate. All those jars in the cottage. None of that knowledge had come from our mother.

But that wasn't what I most wanted to know. "How did you get away? That night—how did you escape?"

Her eyes flashed. "It wasn't me she wanted—little queen."

I winced at the reminder of what our father had sometimes called me. I could not believe she would use it as a weapon, sneering it at me like that. "That wasn't my fault." Gods, why did I say that? What I wanted to say was, *I'm sorry. Please forgive me. I didn't want to leave you.*

Red said harshly, "No," but I couldn't tell whether she meant to agree or disagree, and somehow it felt like she was responding to my thoughts instead of my words, rejecting them.

I closed my eyes. "Red—"

"Shh!"

My eyes popped open. Red was scanning the trees, alert. I followed her gaze but saw nothing. "What ..."

Then I felt it. The wrongness. The strange pressure and stillness that I had grown so accustomed to around Lyric that I'd stopped noticing it.

Demons. They had found us.

No—he had.

He stood at the top of a ridge, no demon, though the shadows of their kind clung to him, drifting around him like black cobwebs. His antlers showed dimly in the filtered light of morning, the moon above his brow pale and diffused.

"Bregas," I whispered.

"To the cottage—now!"

Red shoved at me. I stumbled into motion, bare feet scrambling through the debris of the woodland floor. Behind me, magic hissed and crackled. When I tried to look back at what was happening, I found Red tight on my heels.

"Faster!" she barked then flung out a hand in our wake as though casting stones. The ground sizzled and smoked to lift a wall of gray behind us, muffling a bellow that was half man, half stag.

The cottage came into sight, and I raced for the gate, slamming into it then fumbling with the latch. I got it open and stumbled through onto the path. Red slammed the gate shut behind us. She passed me on the way to the cottage, flying up the steps and through the doorway.

Inside, Red barked a word toward the hearth. Fire burst under the cauldron, which still hung from the chimney chain with the remains of last night's soup. Red growled through a spell I could not follow, the words foreign and harsh. Fog exploded from the cauldron, shooting straight up the chimney, its scent tinged with onions and garlic.

Red's spell grew sharper and more desperate. Stalking around the cottage, she howled, "Move! Curse your wicked old bones—*move*!"

I skittered back from her as she stomped past me, fury transforming her face as much as the crone's withered skin had done. The haze outside the window caught my eye, and I ran over to see the yard obscured by thick fog. I could hear the chickens clucking and shrieking but couldn't see them. The goats bleated in alarm.

Red cursed and glass shattered. I spun to see a puff of brown in the air and a glitter of glass on the floor. At the other end of the cottage, Red snatched another jar from the shelf and hurled it after the first. It exploded against the wall in a cloud of green powder.

"I hate you!" she screamed before sinking down, her back to the wall, her hands hanging limply over her drawn up knees. After a moment, she met my wide-eyed stare and muttered, "I didn't mean you."

"Who did you mean then?"

"The house," she said. "It won't move for me. It refuses."

"Are we … safe?"

"For now. The fog will hide us. The gate will keep him out. Or it *should*. I don't trust this place." Her sapphire eyes locked on me. "We have to kill him."

"No."

She sneered. "Don't be a fool."

"He's bound against his will."

"What does that matter?"

I could only stare. Rose had been a sweet and gentle child with an easy laugh. She had been the one to reach out and take my hand. She had been like summer sunlight.

She sniffed and looked away. Then she pushed to her feet and went to the door. She spoke without looking back at me. "I need to check the perimeter and the animals. There's no telling where that cursed goat has got to. Stay here."

I felt useless. I *was* useless. My little sister was protecting me. My little sister whom I should have been saving—whom I should have saved years ago. Everything about this was upside down. A fist clenched around my heart, and my throat went tight. So I made myself busy.

I was still sweeping up the powders and broken glass when Red returned and kicked off her boots. Swinging her cloak from her shoulders to expose her simple shift and slim figure, she hung the cloak on its peg. She went to the alcove and pulled the curtain shut behind her, emerging a minute later in a shapeless brown dress.

Rose had been a child of lace and frills. Blood Red was someone else. She filled a kettle with water and stuck it in the fire under the cauldron. Then she went about gathering food for breakfast while I finished cleaning up her mess.

When we sat to eat porridge with raspberries and walnuts, I watched her drizzle swirl after swirl of honey into her bowl.

She stilled, honey dripping into her porridge. "What?"

"I guess at least one thing hasn't changed."

She scowled. "What is that supposed to mean?"

I almost said, *Never mind*, but instead reminded her, "You always had a sweet tooth."

She thunked the spoon back into the honey jar. "And *you* always ate butter like it was chocolate."

"Really? I don't remember that." I did like butter, but the years in Thistledown had taught me to use it sparingly.

She snorted with derision. "Of course you don't."

She seemed to take my words as a deflection, but the truth was that I didn't remember a lot about myself from before … Well, from *before*. Some things had come back during my time at the castle with the other girls. The thought gave me a pang.

Dead. All dead except Sorsha, who would only survive by becoming as awful as Lyric—if even that could save her.

And all of it because I had not acted sooner. Because I didn't know what to do. Because I didn't have enough power. What had been the use of my father's lessons about governance if I lacked the strength to apply them?

Then there were the things Lyric had said of him. I could not escape the doubt she'd planted in me, the fear that my mother had been unhappy without my knowing it.

"Stop it," Red said harshly.

I blinked her into focus. "Stop what?"

"Doing that."

I had no idea what she meant.

She gave me a contemptuous look. "You think I can't see all that guilt on your face, like everything in the world is your fault?"

My jaw hardened. "You wouldn't understand." I was the oldest. I was the heir. Father had schooled me in the meaning of that from the time I could walk.

"I understand that it's ridiculous. It shows how little *you* understand the world."

"And you do? Hiding out here in the woods?" It wasn't fair. She had been in the war camp, risking herself. She knew many, many things—dark ones, which she had learned somewhere. I was the one who had hidden for so long. In Thistledown. Behind my scarred face. But I could not forgive her for hiding from me. "Did you know I was alive?"

"No," she said then accused, "You think I'm lying."

"I don't know what to believe anymore. How did you fool me? That was no illusion."

Red smashed a raspberry into her porridge. "I know magic you cannot imagine, that you wouldn't want to."

"And where did you learn all that?"

"Here."

I cast a look around the simple cottage. "I don't understand."

She shrugged.

"You said the cottage wouldn't move for you. What did you mean? What is this place?"

"My home," she said mulishly.

I scrubbed at my face in frustration. "You make me want to—"

"Throttle me? I'd like to see you try." When I gave her a hard look, she sniffed and looked down at her porridge, stirring it but not eating. After a while, she repeated what she'd said earlier. "We have to kill him."

"No."

"Why are you protecting him? Is he your lover?"

My face heated. "Of course not." I'd barely spoken to him. And I'd never had a ... lover.

"Then why—"

"It's *wrong.*"

Red burst up from the table. "How can you be so naïve? You, with half your face burned off?" I froze at her words, and so did she. "I didn't ... I didn't mean that like it sounded. I'm—"

"Don't tell me you're sorry—you're not. And it had nothing to do with you anyway."

Crossing her arms tightly, Red paced around the cottage, turning at the hearth, where the cauldron still poured its fog up the chimney, then turning again at the larder door. She halted by the window, staring out into the haze.

She said, "We'll have to bind him then."

"Is that possible?"

"With Lyric's chain, yes." She glared at me over her shoulder. "Which you wanted me to leave behind, remember?"

Actually, I had wanted it destroyed, but she had a point that I'd given no thought to its future use. It was an evil thing. But if it meant sparing Bregas's life ...

I asked, "How do we catch him to bind him?"

"We lure him."

"Lure him with what?"

Red returned her gaze to the fog beyond the glass. "With you."

I crouched by a stream whose path had carved a cleft in the woods, leaving the ground to rise, rocky and scrubby, a good fifteen feet on either side. I didn't like how the location felt like it trapped me, but the water, Red claimed, would carry my scent through the woods and draw Bregas to me. And the surrounding elevation made it possible for her to wait out of sight, hidden by stones and trees.

The trap wasn't for me, I reminded myself, but for Bregas. I was only the bait.

It wasn't a comforting thought. I hated the sense of powerlessness, but it seemed to be my lot these days. Everyone around me had more power. Lyric. Red. Bregas. The demon horde. And Kraxikel, of course. Though further in the background, he was perhaps the most dangerous of all.

If I let myself think about it, I understood the temptation to bargain for power. Helplessness is a terrible feeling.

I wasn't helpless, though. My magic might not be enough for me to prevail, but it was enough to let me fight.

Fight and die? Perhaps. But I had accepted that from the beginning, had expected Lyric to kill me. In truth, I'd already lived longer than I had thought to. We get greedier, I suppose, as we get stronger. Hope makes us want more.

Trailing my fingers through the clear, shallow water, I watched it ripple. I'd not had much of a chance to test my magic, not this new form of it. A thin sheet of ice spread out around my fingertips, glassy and smooth. Like a mirror, it reflected my face back to me. The water moving below the ice rippled the image, blending my whole face into ruin.

You, with half your face burned off.

I withdrew my fingers from the ice, shattering its thin skin, dispelling the image.

A faint buzzing sound wrenched me from my thoughts. I scanned my surroundings but saw only the stream and rising banks and the yellowing woods of early fall. I felt nothing of that demonic wrongness and yet I sensed *something*.

I caught a flash of blue wings from the corner of my eye. My head whipped around—

Bregas, clad in his green tunic and brown leather, stood upstream, the direction that Red was supposed to be.

"Bregas," I called loudly, meaning, *Red! Get over here!*

She did not appear.

Sunlight spilled down through the canopy, bleaching Bregas's antlers nearly out of sight. Shadows drifted from their ghostly tines like trailing cobwebs. His face was empty. It wasn't Bregas who stalked toward me; it was the Hunter.

"Fight her," I pleaded, not knowing if it was even possible, still unsure whether our quiet moments in Lyric's tent had been real, still unsure of the meaning behind all the actions that had made me ... what? Care about him? Want ... him?

"*No*," he said, as he always did.

"No, what?" I asked, stalling, pleading silently for Red to appear.

Bregas's pale sword shimmered into existence in his hand, the weapon wrought from antler or bone or some Fae magic perhaps. I glanced up the slope again and found it stubbornly empty. Red wasn't coming. Somewhere in the distance, I felt that demonic wrongness, the strange pressure and stilling silence of them.

I tried to call ice to my fingers but managed only a pulsing chill. I didn't want to hurt him. It might be Lyric striking out at me with his hands, but it would be him I had to harm to protect myself.

"Stop," I pleaded, extending a hand. He would leave me no choice but to choose between us. No. *Lyric* would leave me no choice.

Bregas did stop—but not at my words. His head turned, his gaze arrowing up the slope. Demons came skittering along the ridge. Clad in black, with pale faces, they moved like insects despite their roughly human shape. Red appeared suddenly in their midst, hurling magic in sparks and flares. Howling, the demons wheeled on her, and she vanished in their dark swarm.

I bolted through the stream to scramble up the rocky bank. The Hunter surged past me, aiming for Red. I grabbed at him, catching a handful of leather, but he tore from my grasp. I sent a spear of ice after him. He shouted as it ripped across his side, but he kept on up the slope, nimbly leaping from stone to stone, his speed and grace impossible for me to match. He cleared the ridge well ahead of me.

When I reached the top, I found chaos—and Red at the heart of it. Hands slashing, my sister spun among the demons, black smoke spilling from them as they shrieked. Yet against so many—and now the Hunter—we could not prevail.

"Red!" I screamed as Bregas launched into the throng, pale sword sweeping—but not at her.

He slashed through the neck of a demon and sent its head flying. Roots snapped out from the earth to lash and strike and hurl the demons away.

A demon skittered up to me, snatching with long fingers. It screamed when I froze its hands then went silent as I froze its face.

I lacked Bregas's strength and skill. I lacked my sister's focus and control. I could only strike out with sloppy brutality. I speared a demon through the groin. I froze the arm of another and shattered it.

I had no attention to spare for Red or Bregas, except to mark them at the edge of my vision, alive and fighting. How long Bregas would side with us, I could not guess. His fight was two-fronted: against the demons and against Lyric's control of him.

White-hot pain raked my back. I screamed and fell. The demon crawled over me, hissing and clicking, its long tongue snaking out between rows of sharp teeth—then a pale sword pierced its throat, and the thing collapsed into shadow and black smoke.

Bregas stood over me, his expression emptying, his eyes going blank, his pale sword tight in his fist. Shadows wreathed the faint outline of his antlers, dimming the light that shone between them.

"*No*," he breathed, the word small and hopeless this time.

"Bregas." My voice was thin with pain, but his eyes flickered at his name. "Bregas."

I reached out my hand to him, as I had done in Lyric's tent. His eyes began to clear. His grip on the sword began to loosen.

Like the lash of a whip, Lyric's thin silver chain wrapped hard and fast around his neck. The chain had been a mere foot in length when it had coiled around my throat, but now it stretched to several meters, stringing tight from Bregas's throat to Red's fist. She yanked him off his feet. Crashing to the ground, Bregas bellowed like a wild, wounded animal and clawed at his throat as Red chanted, low and harsh, in her strange, foreign tongue.

Vines burst from the ground, snapping toward Red, but somehow she turned them on him. They lashed around him, pinning him down. Thorns sprang up from the vines, piercing and cutting as they bound him, twining even through his fading antlers. Bregas shouted and thrashed. His sword had vanished.

"Stop! Red, stop!"

"It's better this way," she said harshly, her hand clenched on the silver chain, her eyes hard and merciless on Bregas as the vines tightened.

"Red—*stop*."

Her blue eyes lifted to mine. "This is our chance, Snow. To take something from her."

It was the first time she'd said my name since I had learned her identity. She wanted us to be united in this. But I could not accept it. "He is nothing to her but a tool. But to me, he is a person. Stop hurting him."

Red's shriek of rage had me jumping back, ice sparking along my fingertips. She flung the chain into the dirt and aimed a furious finger at me. "He could have killed you! He still could!"

"She's right."

I spun at the tight, pained words. From within the cage of thorny vines, with the silver chain constricting his throat, Bregas gazed out at me, his hazel eyes clear. "You should kill me," he said. "While you can."

"No."

Behind me, Red made a sound of disgust.

"If she takes me again—"

"I won't let her."

"A lovely sentiment," Red snapped, "but what do you mean to do with him?"

"I don't know!" I snapped back. "You agreed to this, Red—did you plan to betray me the instant you had him bound?"

"*Betray* you?" she echoed furiously.

"You agreed to *help*."

"Just let her kill me," Bregas choked out. "She's ... at the edge of my mind."

"Bind him," I ordered Red. "You said you could."

"I said I *might* be able to."

"And yet so far you've tried nothing but killing him."

She glared at me then snarled, "Get out of the way."

I had no choice but to trust her. Red picked up the end of the long silver chain. At a whisper from Red, the vines uncoiled, their constriction loosening, their thorns drawing free to leave spots of blood all over Bregas's skin and clothes.

Red never looked at him, only crouched there in that cloak the color of an old bloodstain, and stared at the wicked chain. She began a quiet incantation. Tendrils of black smoke curled from her mouth and spilled down along the chain, twining around it, weaving through its tiny links. Bregas gasped and choked. Veins threaded along his throat and into his face.

"Red," I whispered, afraid she was killing him after all.

She chanted relentlessly over the chain. The black smoke, disturbingly similar to the demonic shadows, slipped along it to encircle Bregas's neck. His eyes rolled back in his head, and his body started convulsing.

"*Red.*"

She released the chain, and it retracted into itself until it was only a thin ring around Bregas's neck, as it had been around mine. Only now it was not silver, but black.

Red fell onto her rump, shuddering. "We can only hope," she said weakly, "that Lyric will not find him through that."

I dropped to my knees beside Bregas. He had lost consciousness. "And what is 'that'?" I demanded of my sister—this stranger with her dark and unsettling ways. My fingers hovered over the black chain, not touching it.

Red shook her head. "Something I pray you never know."

13.

Strange Company

She's your goat. You milk her."

Red thrust the pail at me. We were walking across the yard on our way to do chores.

After whatever Red had done to Bregas, he'd roused enough to stumble through the woods to the cottage. He was sleeping in Red's bed at the moment. I'd pushed him over there in spite of Red's scowling disapproval. It was her bed, yes, but I wasn't going to drop Bregas on the floor. Not that he would have noticed; he'd passed out cold upon hitting the mattress.

I had wanted to discuss the situation. Red had not.

So here we were.

I clutched at the pail. "We don't *know* it's Prickle."

Basket swinging from the crook of her arm, Red tromped her way to the chicken coop, ignoring me.

"*Red.*"

She spun, braid whipping through the air, sapphire eye flashing. "It's *Blood* Red."

I stared her down. Terrifying she might be, but she *was* my little sister. And she had given in to me, had done as I'd demanded by binding Bregas instead of killing him. She had let me bring him through her gate and into her house, even into her bed. I would not now cower at her snapping temper. And yet, confronted suddenly with her searing, undivided attention ... I found I had both too much and nothing at all to say.

"Never mind," I muttered.

Grumbling, Red swung back toward the rickety chicken coop with its weatherworn slats, and I went my own way to the goat pen.

It was Prickle. I knew as soon as she kicked over the empty pail. She had weaned the kids, and it was late in the season. She was tired of giving milk and she let me know it.

I couldn't imagine how she'd found her way here or why, the uncanny creature, but I had bigger mysteries to solve, so I snatched the half-full pail out of Prickle's range when she aimed a second kick and decided enough was enough. The sudden movement wrenched at the slash down my back. Untying Prickle from the fence, I shooed her off irritably. She trotted to her shed and chased one kid then the other away from the hay.

In the cottage, I found Red leaning over the table and grinding something in a stone mortar. Her eyes flicked to me then back to her work. Still angry with me, then. I walked past her to take the milk into the larder. When I emerged, Red was stirring whatever she'd been grinding into an ointment.

"Sit," she ordered. "This is for your back." When I halted, she misread my surprise as distrust and added crossly, "It won't hurt you."

"That's not what I—never mind."

I went to sit in the chair, my back to her. I loosened the bodice of my frock. Her frock, rather, lent to me. The wound tugged painfully as I extracted my upper body. I slid my shift down as well, clutching the fabric against my breasts.

The ointment stung as Red smeared it across the wound, its bite sharp enough to make me hiss. But by the time she was done and I was sliding my garments back into place, the sting had already cooled and my pain was fading to a dull ache.

"Thank you," I said earnestly, letting her hear my relief, wanting her to understand that I saw the kindness she was showing me.

She only sniffed.

When sounds of movement came from the alcove, I turned in my chair to see Bregas sitting on the edge of the bed, head hanging.

Red thumped the jar of ointment into my hand. "*You* can deal with him." When I blinked at the jar, she added, "He's *all* yours."

"He's not ..." *Mine*. "Oh, fine."

As I got up, Red pointed to a steaming bowl of water and a clean cloth at the end of the table. I gathered these up and carried everything to the alcove.

"Hello," I said lamely.

Bregas looked up. There was no sign of his antlers. He looked almost human, except for the tips of his ears poking through the brown waves of his hair and his astonishing beauty. Even pale and drawn with pain, his face had all those perfect angles: the high cheekbones and well-cut jaw, the finely shaped lips and straight nose, the deep and thoughtful eyes, finally his own.

A few things undercut his inhuman perfection: the blood crusting his skin and staining his clothes. His sorrow. And that black chain around his neck, of course.

"Hello," he replied, revealing his sharp incisors. I had forgotten about that. Another not-human detail.

I had always been the pragmatist, my sister the dreamer. Yet this High Fae intrigued me, drew my eyes in a way no man had ever done. His beauty and mystery. His otherness. His strength.

My interest made me feel awkward. *He's all yours.*

Bregas reached for the things I'd brought. "I can—"

"Remove your tunic please."

I went to set everything on the trunk at the foot of the bed. I had tended Halen's ailments in the past. A smashed finger. Broken ribs after a horse had kicked him. Poison ivy. This would be no different.

I was wrong. It was very much different.

Bregas might not be human, but his physique was far too male—and far too interesting to my eyes. To make matters worse, the wounds were everywhere and that meant my hands were everywhere. He smelled of blood and smoke but also of the deep woods. An earthy scent, tinged with musk and brightened by new green things.

He had some deeper gouges like the one on my back, wounds from fighting the demons. He had risked terrible punishment to help us; he had risked death. We would not have prevailed without his defiance of Lyric.

As Red's ointment eased his pain, his grace returned. I hadn't realized until then how it had left him: the fluid, almost dancelike movement. It made me freshly self-conscious of my hideous scar. His haunted eyes, however, told me had scars of his own, even if they weren't visible. For years and years, Lyric had hurt him. I still wanted to know how she had ensnared him, but I wasn't comfortable asking. I didn't know how to start talking to someone like him. And there was Red in the background doubling my self-consciousness.

Is he your lover? she had asked.

When I had finished his upper body, he said, "Thank you. I can manage the rest."

I shot to my feet and hurried to the curtain, whipping it shut behind me as I made my escape. Red looked up from stirring the cauldron. She lifted an eyebrow.

"Mead?" she suggested.

I stilled my restless hands. "Yes. Please. Yes, that would be good."

She left the cauldron and went down into the larder, returning a moment later with three brimming pottery cups. She set one on the table, handed me another, and kept one for herself. I took a hearty drink. That red eyebrow lifted again.

"What?" I demanded.

"Oh, nothing."

I scowled then nearly jumped out of my skin when Red's mouse suddenly peeked out from the neck of her shapeless dress. The mouse squeaked something. Red snorted.

Rude.

I asked, "Will she find us?"

The last of the fog had lifted, and the cauldron was now emitting the savory steam of mushroom soup instead of magic.

"We cannot hide forever," Red replied darkly, not answering my question. "She knows we're both alive. She must know by now that we have the Hunter."

"His name is Bregas."

Red's lips twitched into a frown, and she walked away, returning to the cauldron. She had wanted to kill him. Maybe that was easier for her to stomach if he was only "the Hunter."

When the curtain was pulled back and Bregas emerged from the alcove, I handed him the third cup of mead. He stared at it.

"You do … um …" Drink? Eat? I knew nothing of his kind. Maybe he subsisted on air and sunlight. But there were stories, I recalled, of the wild feasts in the Brightwood.

He accepted the cup. "Thank you."

"It's my mead," Red pointed out from the hearth.

Bregas walked over to her and inclined his head. "Thank you, Rose Red."

"It's Blood Red," she corrected, not looking at him.

Bregas didn't balk at the name as I had. "Thank you, Blood Red. For your hospitality. And for this." His fingers went to the black chain around his neck.

Red frowned. "Hardly something to be thankful for. You cannot use your magic."

She hadn't told me that, and I did not care for the revelation.

"I have not been able to use my magic for seven years," he said harshly. "*She* has been using it. So I am thankful."

Red paused in her stirring and looked at him, really looked at him for the first time. Nothing in her softened, but she did nod, accepting his words. "You will tell us your story."

He stiffened but said, "Yes."

Red nodded again and returned her attention to the cauldron, the message clear: *Later.*

We ate mushroom soup and bread baked in the hot cubby beside the fireplace. We drank mead. The cottage felt very different with three instead of two. Four, really, if the mouse counted. It kept peeking out from the folds of Red's dress and squeaking its opinions to her. Opinions she seemed to share, judging by the private smile that would tug at the corner of her mouth. Then there was that watchful spider web in a high corner.

This place was old, much older than Red. She had said the house wouldn't move for her, so it possessed magic of its own. How had she come to be here? How had she learned so much magic, and so much of it dark?

Not all of it dark. My back felt almost healed, and the slashes and punctures had all but vanished from what I could see of Bregas's skin.

Where Red's healing was craft, the times Bregas had healed me had been different, something innate in him, something he could no longer access with the black chain around his neck.

Dark and awful as that spell had been, he regarded it as a gift, a protection. It was, I guess. I should have thanked Red for it, as he had.

What was wrong with me?

Why was I so angry with her?

Following supper, when Red had refilled our cups and the woods had grown dark outside the cottage, Bregas told his story.

After Lyric had taken Cresilea by witchcraft and murder, she and her demons had tried to take the Brightwood by force. Bregas had fought outside the boundary of the Fae kingdom, he and a dozen other High Fae, along with thousands of the lesser faeries. The other High Fae had been slain in the battle, but Bregas had been taken alive. He spoke little of what happened after. He'd known only darkness and cold, and the endless torment of whispering magic that invaded his mind until little remained of his own thoughts.

Sitting on the sheepskin rug, knees drawn up to my chest, I rubbed my arms for warmth. It was a terrible story, and the bleak, haunted look in Bregas's eyes told me what a small fraction of that terror he was sharing.

"I'd given up trying to fight her," he said quietly, staring into the fire. He was also sitting on the rug but not beside me. To speak of these things, he needed his own space, I think. In her rocking chair, Red had long since stilled. "Then ..."

"Then what?" I prompted as he trailed off.

He continued staring into the flames. "Then a young woman with more courage than sense forced me to choose her."

"Oh. You knew who I was?"

"Yes. And I knew she would know. I tried not to choose you."

"It would only have been another girl."

His eyes closed. He'd chosen many girls over the years, girls who had been murdered, whose magic had been eaten. He said, "I tried to warn you with the kerchief. I wanted you to know that I'd sensed your magic, that she would too, that she would know you."

"I didn't understand." And it wouldn't have mattered anyway. I had chosen to be there. Even now, I did not regret it.

"I couldn't ... *speak*."

"I'm sorry," I said, knowing it wasn't enough. "For what she did to you."

He looked at me at last, his eyes intent. "You don't need to be sorry for what others have done."

"That," Red interjected, "is an affront to my sister's sense of duty, don't you see."

I ignored her scorn as though I didn't notice it, as though it didn't hurt me. I asked Bregas, "Why did Lyric attack the Brightwood?"

"There's powerful magic among the Fae. She sought to seize it if she could, destroy it if she couldn't." His expression darkened and his tone grew bitter as he said, "If more of the Fae had been willing to fight, we might have destroyed her."

"Why didn't they?" Red asked.

"My father doesn't care for mortals," Bregas answered flatly. "He warned me that he would close the Brightwood behind me if I went to fight. He said it was a human problem and not our concern."

I knew little of the High Fae, but if Bregas's father had the power to close the Brightwood, that meant ... "Is your father the ...?"

"King," Bregas confirmed bluntly.

"Your *father* is the High Fae king?"

"He has many children. I'm only one of them."

He misunderstood my shock. It wasn't that he was royal. It was that his father had such power and had done nothing to help his own child. What did it matter if there were many children? My father would have protected me, would have tried to at least. Despite all that Lyric had made me fear about him and my mother, *that* I knew to be true.

I pressed, "And your father allowed this to happen to you?"

"He warned me, and the Fae cannot lie, so I knew the consequences."

Ice crackled along my fingertips. "That's terrible."

Bregas's eyes softened as he looked at me. "I made my choice."

"*You* chose to fight. *He* chose to abandon you."

When Bregas winced, Red said, "Maybe you don't need to put so fine a point on it?"

"Oh," I said. "Sorry."

"You only speak the truth," Bregas replied grimly. "But he had more to think about than me. You're a queen, Snow. You understand that."

My heart grew heavy with failure. "I'm not a queen."

Red surprised me by saying firmly, "You're the rightful queen."

When I glanced at her, she met my gaze with fierceness and resolve. For the first time since learning her identity, since learning she was alive, I realized that she would fight for me. Not just fight against Lyric, but fight for me. It didn't matter if we were angry or uncomfortable with each other.

Halen had done the same.

Love is not always gentle, nor easy to recognize.

Did Red know that I loved her too, that I was aching with it? I didn't know how to tell her.

I turned back to Bregas and focused on problems instead. That had always been easier for me. "What if we approached your father now? Would he help us?"

Bregas's face darkened, and he said with old, hard anger, "No. He is stubborn. He won't change his mind for a hundred years. By then, it will be too late. Lyric will have summoned Kraxikel into this realm."

"The dwarf I freed said that Lyric wanted his people to make her a crown that would somehow protect her from Kraxikel. She must fear him."

Bregas dashed my fragile hopes. "That fear will not hold her back forever. The more magic she takes"—I heard the word *eats*—"the bolder she grows. She will call him. And when she does …" Bregas looked away into the shadows, seeing a future he dared not speak of.

I looked for possibilities, and found one in my memory. "The dwarf also said that the real craft of his people was truth. He told me to remember it. What if they could make a different kind of crown? Something that would help us?"

"Dwarves are liminal beings," Bregas said, "half demon themselves. They venture deep into the darkness, crossing over as they please. They cannot be trusted."

"Then why did you let that one escape—and bear the punishment for it?"

Bregas looked at me steadily. "Because I trusted you."

My breath caught, and my heart warmed. It was an unfamiliar sensation, one I didn't know what to make of, one that frightened me a little.

Red pointed out, "An object powerful enough to fight Lyric could be dangerous in her hands. In many hands."

"I don't see what choice we have but to seek power beyond what we possess." I didn't like how that idea echoed Lyric's rationale, but the truth of it silenced us all for a moment. Then Red spoke.

"What makes you think the dwarves will help us when they refused Lyric?"

"I don't know that they will," I admitted. "We can only ask. We must at least try."

"We can only ask if we can find them," Bregas pointed out. "The dwarf that Lyric had, Kraxikel had thrust from the demon realm when it delved too deep. The creature never told Lyric how to find the dwarves' mountain home."

"I can find them," Red said then amended, "Well—someone I know can."

I latched onto that. "Good. Unless one of you has a better idea?"

"Who is this person?" Bregas wanted to know.

Red smiled wickedly. "You'll see." With that, she whispered to the mouse, who squeaked and raced down her arm then across the cottage to the door, squeezing under it. "You'll see in the morning."

Red retired to the loft, leaving the alcove to Bregas. Or me. Or, as Red muttered, "You two."

Bregas insisted that I take the bed. It was a strangely mundane argument to have with a High Fae prince.

Somehow, he won. Through his stubbornness, I suppose, or my awe of him.

Despite the down mattress and despite the weariness that had my body sinking into it like a stone, I could not fall asleep. Rising from the bed, I peered around the curtain to see Bregas sitting before the hearth, lost in thought.

It reminded me of the times he had appeared in the shadows of Lyric's tent. Lost, as I had been. Lonely, as I had been.

When I padded over and sat beside him, he said nothing, only looked at me, his hazel eyes beautiful and haunted. I could not imagine what the past seven years had been for him, and I wondered if he really was so fortunate after all to look so perfect. It was too easy to forget his pain when looking at his beauty.

And he was beautiful. Even when I had thought him evil I'd thought him beautiful. And now … knowing how he'd fought her, knowing that he'd been shaped into the Hunter because he'd chosen to fight in the first place? He was all the more beautiful to me.

And I was vain enough to be glad that it was my unblemished side that he saw, the ugly side facing instead toward the shadows.

Quietly, asking nothing, he reached out his hand, offering it to me as I had offered mine to him in Lyric's tent. I took it. His palm was warm and welcome against mine, and I threaded my fingers with his.

At last, my mind settled, and I drifted in the warmth of the hearth and his hand and the sense of being not quite so alone. When I slumped onto my side, Bregas lay down behind me, asking for nothing, offering only his company.

I slept soundly. He must have too because he remained a solid, unmoving presence behind me when I opened my eyes to daylight—and to a short, hairy snout with long, sharp teeth.

Part 3.

Fire and Forge

14.

Matters of Trust

At my scream, Bregas jerked awake behind me. I found myself wrenched across the floor and went tumbling out of the way as Bregas leaped to his feet to face a massive, shaggy bear.

Bregas's hand reached out as though for his sword, but with no magic he had no sword to call upon. I scrambled for my own magic, managing only to freeze the floor beneath me.

"Naughty bear!" Red exclaimed, laughing, as she descended the steep, narrow stair from the loft.

The bear swung toward her, its huge, round rump hitting the table and sending it juddering several feet. Its jaws stretched wide to display gleaming teeth, and its dark eyes twinkled, either with mischief or malice. I was inclined the suspect the latter, but Red didn't seem worried.

A mouse, Red's mouse, emerged from the ruff of thick hair around the bear's neck. It skittered over the crown of the huge animal's head and down between its eyes to its snout. The bear sneezed like thunder, shaking the walls and setting the jars to rattling on their shelves. The mouse went sailing through the air.

"Bear!" Red complained and hurried down the last steps, rushing across the cottage to scoop up her mouse. She scolded the little creature under her breath, "You did rather bring that on yourself."

Bregas's head swung from Red to the bear to me and back to the bear. "Your ... friend?" he asked Red.

"I'm sorry. He shouldn't have startled you two like that. He's very bad."

I didn't think Red was the least bit sorry—and I thought she'd developed far too much liking for the phrase "you two." The bear chuffed, clearly pleased with himself.

When I'd first entered Red's cottage, she had mentioned a bear that sometimes spent the winter here. There had been so much going on that I'd forgotten the comment. We'd been talking about the goats at the time, and Red had said she didn't know what the bear would do when it saw them. Jolted by the thought, I rushed outside.

"Waaaahhhhh!" Prickle screamed from the roof of the cottage.

Red appeared beside me on the path of blue stones. "Get down right now or you won't have to worry about Bear—I'll eat you myself!"

Prickle leaped onto the woodpile, and one of the kids jumped up to join her, head-butting her in the side like it was all a great game. We returned to the cottage to find Bregas standing in the kitchen area eyeing the bear warily as it rubbed its rump against the hearthstones, lips twitching at the relief of an itch well scratched.

I looked to Red. "So ... will he lead us to the dwarves?"

When the bear growled, I stumbled back in alarm, tripping over Red's boots, which were lying by the door. Bregas moved in front of me as though to shield me. Red tracked his movement, sapphire eyes missing nothing. My face heated.

Is he your lover?

Bregas and I shared something, some understanding of darkness and loneliness, I think. Nothing more.

"Don't growl," Red scolded the bear then explained, "He doesn't like dwarves."

Bregas muttered, "A creature of sense, then."

"But he will guide us," Red confirmed, and the bear made a grumbling sound that I hoped was agreement.

Red was no more inclined to explain the mystery of the bear than to explain anything else about her life. We would simply have to trust her. And the bear.

It took several days to prepare for our journey. We could forage and hunt along the way, but some provisions needed to be brought along. Everything went into the cauldron, which never filled, no matter how much was stuffed inside: parcels of food, skins of water, blankets and clothes. The clothes were winter ones, a fact that disturbed me. It was early fall. How long would this journey take?

Red only shrugged and said we should be prepared and that winter came earlier in some places than others. When I asked why we couldn't use the cauldron to travel, she said she could not take us to a place she didn't know.

What took the most time was Red closing up the cottage. This, too, disturbed me, the way she was sealing up the windows and magically bolting cupboards and cubbies that I hadn't even noticed before. She seemed to not expect to return for a long time, if at all.

I didn't question her spells or disturb her as she walked endless patterns around the cottage and sheds, through the yard, and in and out of the gate. The blue stones that led to the porch took on a faint glow and something shimmered in Red's wake as she walked, hissing out magic, her fingers flicking. The goats, silent for once, stayed in their shelter, and the hens huddled in the coop.

While Red worked these final spells, I was standing with Bregas outside the gate. The bear lounged in a patch of sunlight behind us, claws relaxed and eyes half-closed. When Red finished her pattern and came to the gate, she fished the mouse from her pocket and said, "I'm sorry, but it's no place for you." Then she pecked the top of its head with a kiss and set it on the ground.

The mouse looked up at her with tiny, beady eyes, and she said gruffly, "Go on now."

The mouse was skittering up the path of blue stones when the cottage and yard vanished from sight. Red closed an invisible gate and turned to join us.

She looked unhappy to be leaving her home, and I wanted to say something, but she sniffed and turned to the bear and said, "Lead the way."

We traveled all day through the woods at the bear's ambling pace. I knew the woods around Thistledown, but I was no woodsman and could tell nothing about our course. I suspected we were moving northward, but I couldn't locate the sun through the interlacing branches.

Bregas stayed alert as we walked, his eyes tracking shadows, his head cocking this way and that. At one point, when he grew tense and watchful and his lip was curling back from his sharp incisors, I asked, "Is everything all right?"

He jerked like he'd only just remembered he was traveling with me—or anyone. "Huh?"

"Is everything all right?" I repeated, though what I meant was, *Are* you *all right?*

"Yes," he said. "I just keep expecting ... something."

Someone, he meant.

That night, we made a fire for warmth and comfort. It did not comfort me. This was the first campfire I'd been around since Halen had burned me, and it was stirring up old, unwanted feelings. It didn't help that I'd spent all day making sure Bregas was on my right side, my unblemished side. I hated that I did that, but I couldn't stop myself.

When I looked out at the world, I couldn't see the disfigurement. I could feel it, the difference in the skin, the way my facial expressions tugged against it, but I was used to that and rarely noticed. Yet, in the eyes others, I felt myself change from *me* into something else. A burned girl.

Red came over to me, scowling. "Why didn't you say the boots don't fit?" I blinked in surprise. I had worked so hard not to let it show. She rolled her eyes. "Take them off."

I did as Red commanded. Kneeling, she began to slather her ointment on my heels and toes. When the fire popped and made me jump, Red frowned, noticing my reaction as she noticed everything. "How did it happen?"

I couldn't bring myself to actually tell the story, so I only said, "It was supposed to protect me. To hide who I was."

Red thought through that, clearly understanding my implication, that the burn had been deliberate. She had been such a sweet and smiling child that I don't think I ever realized how intelligent she was. I had been the one schooled in facts and figures.

"But it didn't work," she observed.

"Maybe it did. Maybe without it, she would have found me when I was too young to fight her. Maybe someone would have turned me in. *I didn't find a magical cottage in the woods.*" The bitterness that crept into my voice at that last bit surprised me.

Red stilled. "Is that what you think happened to me?"

"How can I know what to think when you've told me nothing?"

"I didn't find the cottage," Red said quietly. She was crouched before me, her back to the fire, her face in shadow. "The cottage found me. Rather, the witch did."

"The witch?"

"She's dead now. I killed her."

Chills raced over my skin, not just at the words but at her blunt, harsh tone. "Did she hurt you?"

Red jolted like she hadn't expected that to be the direction of my thoughts. She had been prepared for hard words between us, for me to judge her. She shifted uncomfortably then grumbled, "Put your boots back on."

"Red—"

"Put them *on*."

When I did as she insisted, she gripped my feet through the leather. I felt the soles lengthen and the leather stretch until the fit was perfect. Though much of her magic unsettled me, a lot was simple and useful. Mine, on the other hand, was a few childhood memories, the little tricks that Lyric had taught, and my unpredictable manifestations of ice. Red's skill made me feel like a clumsy child.

"Thank you, sister," I said as Red pulled back.

She nodded and left me.

Bregas was easier company than Red. Silence was comfortable with him, but so were words. As the days passed and we walked on and on, he began to speak more. I began to suspect that conversation was his way of avoiding his own thoughts, but I couldn't blame him. His thoughts must have been dark and haunted.

Mortal craft fascinated him. Our blankets and tools, our music and stories. Red claimed she couldn't remember our childhood tales, so I was forced to tell them. I was terrible at it, always reporting facts without the details. Red would interject now and then with an obviously clear memory. When I pointed that out one night, she only shrugged and said she liked having me tell the stories.

She had brought a flute and played sometimes in the evenings, her fingers nimble, her body weaving slightly. In the firelight, her eyes shone like sapphires and her hair gleamed like a thousand brilliant rubies. Even hidden in her shapeless dresses and awful cloak, even with the eerie, hulking bear behind her, my sister was utterly beautiful.

The bear would sway to Red's music as though enchanted by her. He vanished sometimes in the night, returning in the morning with blood staining his maw. I accidentally startled him once, and he wheeled on me, feral as a bear could be. He snapped out of it at Red's shout. I learned to avoid him. He was Red's mystery, not mine.

Bregas tried the flute one night, and it sang out music unlike any I'd heard even from Red, even from my father's best court musicians. It didn't seem possible that such a simple instrument could emit such complex, lilting music. We were in a cave that night, warm and cozy inside with the light dancing over rough stones, a chill wind blowing past the entrance.

As Bregas played, a flutter of blue caught my eye. The faeries danced into the cave and over to Bregas. I watched them warily, but Bregas didn't seem concerned. They danced along his flying fingers, as light and lovely as the notes. Some alighted above his head as though clinging to his antlers—antlers that had not been visible since the chain had blackened around his throat. I had almost forgotten them, but if I looked only from the corner of my eye, I could almost see them, faint as a memory.

When Bregas drew the flute away from his lips and the song faded, he held out a hand. The faeries fluttered down onto his palm and crowded up along his arm. He spoke in a language I didn't know, a lovely, melodious one. Despite the beauty of his cadences, his tone carried sorrow. Tears shone in his eyes.

It surprised me. I had never seen him cry, and I couldn't recall the last time I had done so myself. I had often called it strength in myself, that dryness, but as Bregas wept gently for the little faeries, for the evils of the world, something shifted inside me, some understanding, and I suddenly envied him the courage to feel so deeply, to express it. It didn't weaken him at all.

The faeries fluttered from his hand and began to dart around the cave. Without the music to focus them, they reverted to their troublesome ways. One tugged rudely at my hair. Bregas gently shooed it away. Another fluttered unwisely in front of the bear. He snapped at it, jaws missing by an inch, the rush of air sending the faerie tumbling.

"Bear!" Red chastened. He chuffed in annoyance.

As the faeries fluttered out of the cave, Bregas said to me, to everyone, to himself perhaps, "We must fix this."

I asked, "Why are they like that?"

"I'm not sure. When Lyric attacked the Brightwood, when we fought her and she ... took me ... something happened. Some poison or contaminant from the demon realm? Or maybe because they were closed out of the Brightwood? I don't know."

"I'm sorry," I said, unable to escape the sense that I was responsible for what Lyric did. It was my throne she ruled from, doing these things.

"So am I," Bregas replied, sharing the burden with me.

I expected some sneering comment from Red about my sense of duty, but she said nothing.

That night, as the fire burned low, I shifted closer to Bregas. We often lay close at night, arms entwining—and I often wanted something that I didn't quite understand and didn't know how to ask for.

"You're such a fool to waste time," Red said to me the next day.

Snowflakes were spiraling out of the sky. It didn't seem like enough days had passed for winter to be coming, but it was. Here, at least.

"What do you mean?" I asked, but my eyes went to Bregas, who was whittling as he walked, his clever fingers working a knife against a piece of wood.

Red only shook her head.

Not long after that, one of Lyric's winged demons found us. It descended, screeching, from the sky, its leathery wings tipped with cruel talons, its claws extended. It went straight for Bregas.

I didn't even think. I simply felt a sudden, fierce desire to destroy this wicked and hideous thing. It was that cold, terrible part of me that I both loved and hated. Feared, maybe. It was the part of me that Lyric prized, the part of me that wanted to force things to be as *I* wanted. I sent a spear of ice flying with such force that when it caught the demon in the chest, it drove the creature ten feet through the air and nailed it to a tree.

Two more demons streaked down from the sky. The bear leaped for one, claws shredding the demon's leathery wings. Red rushed to help him, magic crackling from her fingertips.

I hurled a spear of ice at the other demon, but the glittering shard flew wide, and the creature tackled Bregas. They tumbled, wrestling viciously. Without magic, Bregas had only his fists and the small knife he'd been whittling with. He was such a fine and gentle male that I'd forgotten he was also a warrior. He had fought demons alongside me and Red not long ago, had been bound by Lyric while defending the Brightwood, and I'd seen him in the aftermath of battle in Lyric's tent many times. Lyric would not have wanted him if he lacked the skills and mind of a warrior. So it should not have been a surprise to see his battle rage rise up, especially at the chance to fight what had so long enslaved him. Still, his brutality shocked me after so many days of his curiosity and music and safe, comfortable arms.

He roared in fury and ripped at the screaming demon; he tore it apart with his bare hands. Soon it was only a smoking ruin, fading in the air and leaving Bregas with nothing but his lingering rage.

When nothing more arrived to trouble us, I approached Bregas cautiously. He was on his knees, his chest heaving, his lips peeled back from his teeth. Someone else might have known what to say or do. I did not, so I simply waited beside him. When his anger had settled, he got to his feet, and we walked to the nearby stream whose course we'd been following.

After scrubbing cold water over his face, Bregas said, "I'm sorry."

"For what?"

He shook his head. "I don't know."

His fingers went to his throat, to the black chain, and I couldn't tell whether he wanted to rip the thing away or whether he was relieved to find it there.

"Has she found us?" I asked.

"If she had, there would have been more. She must have sent scouts everywhere. These happened upon us."

After a while, I asked, "Are you all right?"

His silence was answer enough: *No.*

Nothing was all right, none of this, but when I took his hand, he interlaced his fingers with mine. It wasn't until my fear and aloneness lifted at the touch that I realized how they had stiffened me inside and out. I thought of all those hours in Lyric's tent. I thought of the way it felt when Bregas held me at night.

Magic has power.

Words have power.

And so, I was beginning to learn, does touch.

That night after supper, when the bear wandered off on one of his sojourns, Red went with him. We had a fire to drive back the night's cold. We had no cave, but an overhang of rock offered a semblance of shelter. Bregas and I sat on our bedroll. As always, he wore his green tunic and brown leather trousers and boots. He never seemed to be cold, but I was. I shivered in my cloak.

When Bregas put his arm around me, I scooted closer to him, relieved. I might have grown comfortable reaching out a hand, but I did not know how to do more. I wanted more, though.

He stroked my hair. Then he kissed me.

I had never been kissed, not like that: his lips exploring mine, me tasting the honeysuckle sweetness of him, our tongues entwining. I had never felt anything more foreign. I had never felt anything I wanted so completely and so simply: I wanted him.

He was beautiful, but that wasn't what I saw and felt as he stroked my hair and back, as I hesitantly put my hands on his chest and shoulders, in his hair. It was his depth that I wanted, the way he was so full of emotion and thought, of pain and pleasure, of desire.

He wasn't human. I was always aware of that and never more so than in that moment. I felt the sharpness of his incisors as he grazed them along my neck in a way that made me shiver. I smelled the slight muskiness of the deep woods, the clean brightness of growing things, the otherness of him.

But he was simple in this, letting all other mysteries give way to this one.

Where he was all beautiful fluidity, I was awkward and impatient. I knew there was something to get to, but I didn't know how to ask for it, how to tell him. He drew back a little.

"We'll get to the end," he promised then leaned in once more to kiss along my jaw. He turned me into someone I barely recognized, someone who made a breathy, wanting sound. "Why waste all the delights along the way?"

I knew nothing of what he spoke.

He showed me.

He was slow and careful, always asking, never rushing past any new thing. Sometimes, I felt his trembling. It pleased me that though this might not be new for him like it was for me, it still reached deep into him. But, then, everything did.

Something happened to me that night in his arms, as we lay bare to each other, as I experienced his body—felt it, watched it—and experienced my own in a way I never had. I became someone else in that moment, someone who let another see her, who expressed her feelings in little sounds and movements. That wasn't like me, or so I thought. It took me a long time to understand that none of us are a single thing. We are many things. Different things with different people. I didn't know that at the time.

"Snow White," he whispered later, marveling at my name as we lay entwined, the firelight licking over our joined hands.

The way he said it made me turn my ruined side more into the dark. He said it as though I was beautiful. For the first time in seven years, I could not deny that I wanted to be. I wanted to not have been burned, for Halen to have found another way to hide me.

"Just Snow," I said. Snow, after all, could be many things, not all of them pure and lovely. It could be icy, crusted, dirty. Ugly.

Bregas frowned, and his fingers played with my ebony hair. He might have said, *It's only half your face.* Or he might have said, *It doesn't matter to me.* Or even, *Beauty lies within.* I would know whatever he said to be true to him because he could not lie, but none of it would comfort me. But he said none of those things. He said, "I love you."

It made my heart ache. It made the ice melt. He had never mentioned my scar, not once in all our time together. He never stared at it but never looked away from it either. And when he said those words, he said them to all of me.

I wanted to say it back—I felt it instinctively—but I questioned those words in myself, and so they lodged, unspoken, inside me. I told myself I needed to be sure before saying such a thing, but the truth was that I was afraid of those words. I was afraid they would take my strength from me.

Bregas saw something of my turmoil, though perhaps not the heart of it. "It's all right," he said. "Love doesn't require return in order to exist. It simply is, and I spent so many years silenced that I will not silence myself."

He was so much stronger than me. So much braver.

I didn't understand that until later.

As we kept traveling, Bregas and I found times and ways to be alone, to know each other better. He made me smile, even laugh. I was different with him than with others. I worried about that—that I was changing, weakening, softening—yet I *liked* who I was with him. But only with him.

I was beginning to trust myself with it, to think that perhaps I could be this ... woman ... with him and not lose everything else that I was.

I wanted him to speak of love again. I thought I might now be brave enough to return the words. But he didn't. Perhaps, once voiced, they were real for him. He couldn't lie, after all. What need to repeat a truth already spoken?

But it was so new to me, and I was young and human and inexperienced, full of doubts. I needed his words again, to test myself against them.

Maybe if there had been more time.

Maybe if I hadn't kept thinking of my ruined face and how it looked beside him.

The snow fell harder and faster and no longer melted in the afternoons. It gathered on the ground until we had to trudge through it, the bear leading the way, Red and I wrapped tight in our cloaks. Even Bregas's cheekbones reddened with cold.

The bear was getting harder to wake each morning, and he growled ferociously every time Red shook him. I didn't dare approach him, and even Red grew wary. The bear wanted to sleep, as he was meant to through the winter, but we still needed him.

We had been walking for so long and through such deep woods that when we broke suddenly from the trees one evening and the mountains reared above us, I staggered back into Red. Golden light glowed from within a jagged, wedge-shaped opening. I shivered as I had at the sight of Kraxikel in the mirror, for there was something strange and otherworldly about that entrance.

Bregas had described dwarves as liminal beings, able to cross boundaries, not truly bound to any realm. Their magic followed a similar principle of transition. The dwarf I had freed had called himself a crafter; he said he shaped and remade things. He'd taken heat from my body to light a candle. His riddling nature had annoyed me, but he had seemed incapable of thinking in straight lines, taking ideas from a dozen places to make one thought.

To enter their mountain kingdom, to place our fates in their hands ... I didn't like it, but what choice did we have? And, I wondered, what price would we pay?

That was another thing Bregas had told us of the dwarves: they did nothing for free. Everything was exchange: one thing into another, one thing for another. Transition. Transformation. Transaction.

The bear growled and turned in the blowing snow. I made a sound of protest, but Red shook her head within her shadowed hood.

"He'll go no farther," she said. "It would do us no good in any case, if he ate the first dwarf in sight."

The bear's huge, rounded form disappeared into the trees. Frightening as he'd been, I hated to see him go, to know we were at the sudden end of our journey and now, suddenly, unguided.

"Let us face this," Bregas said grimly.

We trudged on through the snow toward the jagged, spearing mouth of the mountain. The golden light spilled out onto the snow, but there was no invitation in it, no warmth, only strangeness. My skin was prickling, and Bregas was tense as a bowstring beside me. Of Red, hidden within the folds of her reddish-brown cloak, I could tell nothing.

Wind moaned down from the mountains, and the cold bit with cruel indifference. With it came a memory.

You stand at my door, the dwarf had said as I approached his cell in the castle. *Let me out—and I will let you in.*

I don't want in, I had replied, thinking he referred to the cell.

You will, had been his answer. *When the cold bites your bones. When the stones groan and the wind moans—you will.*

I shivered at the cold he'd promised—and at the future he'd seen. The dwarf had known I would come here. He'd told me so but not in a way I could understand. When I had reproached him for his riddling, he'd said, *A riddle is lesson that you learn when you're ready.*

What else had he said? Other warnings, I was sure, but I could dredge up no more from my memory as we ducked through the wind and snow to face the mysteries of the mountain.

"Halt!" called a voice from above as soon as our feet touched the gilded snow. I looked up through the blowing white to see a small, wizened figure crouched among the rocks. "What can a Fae prince and two witches want of the mountain?"

I didn't like that he should know us when we did not know him. I didn't like that another dwarf had foretold our coming. These creatures blurred every boundary, even time. I had been raised by a king on the idea of boundaries and rules. I did not at all like the dwarves' disregard of such things. And yet, that was the very reason we were here, why we needed them.

Red announced our purpose. "We seek your help in destroying a demon."

"And what would you trade for such help?"

"What would you ask?" I called, then added, "Speak plainly."

"Speech is never plain," countered the dwarf before he leaped down from the rocky slope and came trudging through the snow to us. He came only to my waist and had wiry little limbs and a craggy face with a long brown beard that forked into two braided sections. A leather cap crowned his head.

"Who seeks this trade?" asked the dwarf, looking among us.

"I do," both Bregas and I said at once.

I willed the dwarf to look at me. Bregas had paid for me already, perhaps more than once. This was my task and my debt. My problem to solve.

The dwarf looked between us. "You cannot lie, Fae prince, but her truth is stronger. Come." He turned and stumped toward the mountain, motioning over his shoulder with a hand disproportionately large for his body.

We followed him through the snow and up a narrow path to the jagged, gold-lit entrance. I pressed ahead of the others, taking position behind the dwarf. Bregas, whose grace shone forth in all other things, did not show much grace now. He practically shivered with tension behind me. He didn't like this. I didn't care. I was glad of his presence, but this part had nothing to with him. I was alone in my duty and needed to bear the weight of it myself.

We passed through the wedge-shaped entrance into an entry hall of sorts, where torchlight gleamed over jeweled walls. The ceiling, which seemed as high above our heads as the sky, glittered with diamonds, like stars. Stretching ahead, dozens of golden doors, engraved with intricate designs and set with hundreds of gems, stood closed like the lids of jewelry boxes. Our rough, wiry little guide in his simple leather cap looked odd in such grand surroundings.

The dwarf led us to a set of double doors that reared high into a single peak, like a spear point. The doors opened without being touched, and we followed the dwarf into a huge feasting hall.

A hundred tables stood in neat rows, and a thousand dwarves sat eating from silver plates and drinking from finely wrought cups. The scents of roasted meat and yeasty ale hung heavy in the air, and firelight blazed from a dozen huge fire pits. The smoke rose into the darkness overhead. No ceiling was visible here, as though the chamber extended endlessly upward into distant crags and crevices of stone.

Thousands of small, dark eyes watched us enter, and all fell silent. I could not look upon so many, but all seemed to have the small, wiry shape that I had come to know as dwarfish.

Our guide led us past the fire pits and rows of silent feasters to a table set on a dais, where seven white-bearded dwarves with crowns of gold looked down upon us. The one in the center, in the highest chair, looked as ancient as it was possible to be. He was shrunken and pale, but his dark eyes glittered with intelligence and canniness.

"Who is disturbing our feast?" he asked in an old, creaking voice.

"Someone who would drink of our mead?" asked another.

"Someone who would eat of our bread?" asked a third.

"Someone who would ask of us a bed?"

"Someone who would ask of us our craft?"

"Someone who would trade?"

"Someone strong enough to break—and remake?"

This last caught my attention—and my eye. There, at the end of the table was the dwarf I'd set free. In place of his dirty red cap with its long tassel, he now wore a golden crown. His dark eyes twinkled as he saw me recognize him.

Had I seen as he did, across the boundary of time, I would have traded him his freedom for what I wanted now, but I had not known to bargain, and that chance was gone.

"I am Snow White," I said, "and all you say is true." Or so I hoped, though I didn't know what to make of that last question, nor did I much like it. "I've come to you for your craft, as I think you know. I need the strength of the mountain in a silver ring. A crown for a queen."

The oldest of the seven said, "We make things of truth. What truth would we make of you?"

"I think you must answer that."

The old dwarf looked thoughtful. "And what is that worth to you?"

Bregas spoke over me. "I am the son of the Green King. I can bargain with you as she cannot."

"Not true, prince, though you may believe it so," countered the dwarf I had freed. "You are bound and banished yourself. Your worth to us lies in her."

I should have stopped and thought. I should have realized it was a riddle and remembered the dwarf's warning that a riddle is a lesson to be learned. I did none of those things. I demanded, "What do you ask of me?"

My heart pounded, but I was used to enduring. I had endured the maiming of my face. I could endure the loss of my youth or my hair or my voice or whatever remained of my beauty. I would give them years of service. I would give them my life. I could endure any of that if it meant defeating Lyric.

They asked for none of that, but in a way, they asked for all of it, little though I understood it at the time.

"You will give us your loss."

"You will give us your pain."

"You will give us your heart's breaking."

I thought: *I have endured all of that already. I have survived it. I have become what I am because of it.*

I thought, like the world's worst fool: *my heart has grown too strong to break—but that will be their own bad bargain.*

I thought wrongly because I had not been listening. I had been silencing my heart for days, weeks, longer maybe, denying its voice and thinking myself strong. All I did was make myself blind. I did not know what I stood to lose.

Bregas tried to speak, but I said, "Done."

Once upon a time, a girl with a heart of winter tried to speak of love, but the words were frozen inside her. Yet the words still existed, and so they still had power.

Words have power, and no word is stronger than love.

Here is a riddle: if love is silenced, when it echoes, what word does it say?

Once upon a time, a girl learned too late that the word is grief.

"Done."

Who would have thought I could destroy everything with one word?

I had ignored Bregas, had refused to look at him or Red. I had been determined that I would do this, that I would pay the price, that they would stay back from it. It was my loss to endure.

Then I heard Bregas gasp.

Then I smelled burning flesh.

I whipped toward him, but he was already backing away from me. Horror and fear reshaped his face into one I'd never seen. Around his neck, the black chain was glowing— *melting*. And then it was only a ring of smoke that broke apart and faded into nothing.

I let out a wordless, powerless scream as Bregas's face went blank, as his eyes emptied. His crown of antlers shimmered into sight, and the moon rose between them, wreathed in shadows.

The shadows rippled and shivered and coiled around him. Bregas opened his mouth to speak, but he had no words. I had not given my voice—but his.

It was his that was precious to me.

It was *him* that was precious to me.

Another of the dwarf's riddles surfaced in my mind: *All must yield their heart, one way or another.*

I had protected my heart from Lyric, fought against her to keep it. To Bregas, I had given it. And now the dwarves were breaking it.

Bregas whirled away from me, some lingering part of him knowing he must, at least, get away.

Shouting, I ran after him, but my voice echoed in the hall, unanswered, as Bregas stalked away, fading a little more as he passed through each shadow. I lunged for him, desperate, but he faded from my grasp and was gone. I crumpled, weeping, into a wretched pile of travel-stained clothes and weary flesh and misery.

When seven shriveled figures gathered around me, I offered no resistance. They turned my face upward. One set a vial to my cheek, capturing my tears. "Loss," he said.

Another held a box near my chest for a moment then snapped it shut. "The sound of a heart breaking."

The others threw a cloth over me, a shroud perhaps. "Pain," they said.

Then the seven whispered together, "Time will tell what we've unearthed."

15.

The Breaking of Things

I woke in an unfamiliar bed to a view of sparkling silver. It was only an impression, for my swollen and unwilling eyes wanted to see nothing at all. The bed was small, and I was curled up like a child to fit. The sparkle intruded upon my vision, forcing me to see it: a fine mesh curtain hanging around the bed, strange and beautiful. I did not care.

I lay there for hours. Or was it days? I don't think I would have noticed if long years had passed. Perhaps I would remain there, shrinking and shriveling until my hair turned brittle and gray and my skin thinned to a papery husk.

Beyond the shimmering veil, I could sometimes see seven little figures. I felt like I was watching them through a waterfall. I heard them as though in a dream.

"She is still lying in my bed."

"Her heart is still breaking."

"Her pain is yet making."

"Her loss is yet working to shape her."

I might have stayed there forever as though dead had not a hand parted the sparkling curtain. A fine young hand with dirty fingernails and a faint whiff of bitter magic. My sister leaned in, frowning at me, her ruby brows drawn low over sapphire eyes. She was a jewel in a jewelry box here. If she were not so dangerous, I would have feared for her among these grasping and covetous creatures.

If they tried to pluck the blue from her eyes, would she blast and break them, unmake them?

Could she?

Would she?

Would she do it for me?

"You need to eat," she said, as though that mattered. When I said nothing, she scolded, "You cannot give up now. Nothing is finished."

Her words were a whisper amid the howling of my grief.

Red sighed and sat on the bed, the shimmering curtain draping to the side of her and firelight glittering in around her. She looked like a witch from a story, eerie and lovely and full of dark wisdom.

"You were right." My voice sounded like the dry rustle of a forgotten thing, like a ghost.

"About what?"

I could not lift my head from the pillow. "You said I was a fool to waste time."

Red said no word, but I had learned there was power in silence as well, terrible power. *Yes,* said the silence. *You were.* It was harsher than her voice could ever have been.

"I did not tell him that I loved him, and now it means nothing to say it."

Red relented to offer, "I'm sorry," but it was not her doing, not her failing, and I could not hear anything in her words but that.

When I made no reply, Red sighed and left me. The sparkling curtain fell back into place. The curtain was made of tiny links of silver, like the finest chainmail. Astonishing. I think that is why I finally got up. I was tired of its unmoved, unchanging beauty.

I slid from the bed and under the curtain and puddled myself on the floor of a strange chamber. Mine was not the only bed. There were seven in all, each as small and fine and kingly as the one in which I had slept. The floor of the chamber was smooth stone softened by plush rugs and the pelts of huge white bears. The ceiling was low, and the room had the still, silent, closed in feel of being deep underground. It was cold and dim, the only light coming from a single candle on the table.

It felt like a tomb.

Rising on shaky legs, a white nightgown billowing around me, I walked to the empty hearth. A broom stood beside it, and I swept the stone floor where ash had scattered. Then I unearthed the banked coals and built a fire and crumpled before it.

Bregas was gone, enslaved again, suffering again. Because I had loved him. Because I had silenced that love in myself. Because I had not understood it.

A witch's power lies in her heart, but maybe that is true for everyone. So lightly had I offered mine to be broken—and Bregas with it.

There were things to think about beyond that, but I could not gather those thoughts. I was empty. Hollow.

But that's not quite right. Only something whole can be hollow. When something is broken, the pieces lie fragmented. Whatever had been held inside spills out. Nothing is *gone*. It is simply useless, like honey dripped into the dirt.

I went to the door, a door of silver and gold, of etching and inlay, another beautiful and unfeeling thing. It opened at my touch, and I walked out into a little antechamber with another hearth and seven glittering little chairs before it. They all stood empty, the dwarves absent. I went through another door, one of gold and emeralds. This one opened into the high-ceilinged maze of the mountain. There were many paths and many doors. It was a place of cold stone and crackling fire, of precious metals and glittering gems and small, strange creatures. A place of ponderous weight and chill, dark mysteries.

From deep in the mountain, I could hear the distant clink of hammers and the faint cadence of song. I followed the sounds down a long, long hallway. In the distance, light blazed through a gigantic opening far out of proportion with the tiny dwarves. As I drew near, the sound of hammering intensified, and the eerie song swung out pendulously in harsh, grating voices.

Heigh! Ho!
Fire, dance and glow! Silver, melt and flow—heigh-ho!
Heigh! Ho!
Mountain, crack and groan!
Hammer, shape and hone! Chisel, break the bones—heigh-ho!
Heigh-ho!
Heigh!

Ho!

Heigh-ho!

I reached the yawning entrance and looked down upon a vast chamber. It was craggy and rough, a place of coarse, broken stone. Firelight flared and flashed throughout the space, a hundred fires of craft, and every precious little secret of the earth glittered around it in a rainbow of colors.

It struck me that the finest and most precious beauty must be dug and broken from dark and secret places. Nothing glitters like a jewel—but nothing glitters without light. That is craft, I guess, to reshape, repurpose, remove.

Is it creation?

Is it destruction?

A thousand voices were singing and a thousand hammers were ringing. Some hammers and picks cracked against stone, chipping away at the mountain; others clinked against anvils. Wheelbarrows trundled about, pushed by sooty dwarves stripped to their waists, their beards of white or brown or red or gold knotted up at their chins, little leather caps on their heads. They went in and out of dozens of tunnels branching off from the cavern.

Some of the dwarves worked at tables with miniature tools or polishing cloths. Steam burst and hissed from barrels as hot metal was plunged in.

Heigh!

Ho!

Crack! Clink! Clank! Glow!

Fire, burn and blow—heigh-ho!

Heigh-ho!

A rocky slope took me down into the cavern. Small, dark eyes darted to me as the dwarves worked, but none spoke to me. I drifted among them like a ghost in my white nightgown, yet there was something fitting about it. This was a place of breaking open, of melting and burning, of destruction. I was all those things. A burned and melted creature that had cooled into something hard—only to be shattered.

Destroyed.

Maybe something could be made again. Or maybe I was like the metal shavings and shards littering the floor, stepped on and forgotten.

When their day was done, the dwarves dropped their tools and jewels and wheelbarrows. They left their worktables and forges and bellows and steaming barrels. They marched up the slope and through the yawning mouth of the cavern. I trailed after them, following them to their feasting hall. I stopped at the door, my heart pounding. It surprised me. I did not know a broken thing could feel.

Someone appeared at my side. It was Red. Her face was dirty and so were her clothes, as though she had delved into the mountain's dark body, crawled through its gritty veins to be covered in its blood.

Blood Red.

I was beginning to understand her chosen name. I was beginning, a little, to understand her. Or maybe I was simply learning to stop expecting her to be the ten-year-old girl I remembered.

There was an empty space at a table, the only space where all else was full. It was a space for two people. For us. I walked with Red, and we sat at the table. Red filled my plate with bread and meat, and she filled my cup with ale.

I didn't touch any of it until she gave my arm a fierce pinch and said, "Don't be so selfish."

There again, at the edge of my mind, were all those things I needed to think about, but the most I could do was try to please her. I picked up my cup and drank the ale, though I could not taste it. I ate the food, though it meant nothing to me.

The dwarves sang and danced and feasted. The seven sat at their high table. The one at the end, the one I had freed, watched me all the night.

Treacherous creature. Maybe if my heart had not been broken, I would have hated him.

When everyone left the feasting hall late in the night, I refused to move. I would stay here, close to where I'd lost him. My eyes kept going to the spot where he had vanished into shadow.

Red gave up on me with a sigh.

I did not quite understand my own pain. Was it loss? Was it guilt? Was it regret for what might have been, what should have been—for what I should have done?

Grief, I think, is all those things.

I found myself wandering again. I didn't know how much time had passed or where I was in the mountain.

I found a cavern very different from the mines, this one dim and warm and damp. The walls glowed faintly with no discernible source of light, and a web of silver lines crisscrossed through it. A pool filled the center of the cavern, and there were heaps of dirty clothes and cakes of soap. I set to work washing.

It felt good to work. I knew how to wash, and when I thought to mend a tear in a pair of little trousers, I found a needle and thread at hand. I don't know how long I was there. Hours maybe, or days. It didn't matter. My hands turned red and rough, but the clothes turned clean and fresh.

All making is destruction, I guess, the yielding of one thing into another, one ruin for another renewal. My face was no different. Beauty ruined, transformed into protection—for the scar was protection, even if Lyric had known me in spite of it. It had been seven years of shielding, not just my identity but my very self. It had divided me from others, had let me hold them away.

Even Bregas.

Even now. There was something about the hard, pitted skin that made me able to hide behind it, to say, *I am separate*.

But I could not be separate. I had things to do. There was a reason I was here.

I scrubbed, and with the rhythm of the work, thoughts began to return: simple understanding that came with simple action. I didn't even know it was a plan that was forming. It was simply one little certainty after another; it was all the pieces that had always been there, reshaping.

I hung each little garment on one of the silver cords that stretched through the chamber like spider silk. As they dried, they vanished. Eventually, there was nothing left to wash but myself.

Despite my hours by the pool, this was the first time I actually looked into it. I saw my own reflection, face scarred on one side, smooth on the other, hair bedraggled and dirty, nightgown damp with sweat and the chamber's humidity.

Slowly, another image overlaid itself with mine, turning my eyes into glowing coals, turning my lips black and awful.

Washerwoman ... sssservant of dwarvesssss?

"And what would you have me be?" My voice creaked like an old hinge.

Steam rose from the pool as Kraxikel's pale, angular face solidified under the water's surface. His black lips stretched and parted in a wicked smile, revealing the jagged sharpness of his teeth.

I would make you powerful—powerful enough to shape this world to your will.

"My will? Or yours?"

I want only to see power used. You would use it. Wouldn't you? Wouldn't you like to set your own rules and boundaries—to see your justice done?

I said nothing and didn't need to. He knew he was right.

Kraxikel's eyes pulsed bright with greed, and one spiderlike hand reached out, breaking the water's surface, the fingers too long and weirdly jointed, tipped with black claws. After a moment, his hand turned to steam and faded from sight.

I stared into the pool, the fire brightness of his eyes burning in mine.

I would use power. That, I had come to understand of myself. I did not like being powerless, helpless, hopeless. I did not like that others shaped things around me. I did not like to be used in their makings. The demon king had seen that in me long before I saw it in myself.

It was why he wanted me.

Lyric was mad, and the things she did, she did because there was pain in her and she wanted someone to pay. She wanted the world to pay. I knew that because I understood it, because I felt it too—toward her. I wanted her to pay for what she'd done. But that was only a part of what I wanted.

When Lyric spoke of a thousand kingdoms, I didn't want the destruction she craved, didn't want to see my pain echo through the world as she did. But there was a part of me that thought: I could do that rightly.

I could rule better.

I would be just.

I would be righteous.

I would be good.

That was what Kraxikel wanted in me: my ambition. My pride. Those, he could manipulate. I had already seen how principles could twist into something awful. He would twist me. He would take justice and contort it. No—he would contort *me* until my justice meant something that pleased him. I *knew* that. And yet ... I felt the draw of power, the temptation to say, *I can best him.*

You are tempted, Snow White, he observed, smiling his wicked smile, his sharp teeth gleaming.

"You would ruin justice. You would invert it."

I seek only an ear—that is all a demon wants. The choices would be yours.

I could see how it would be: him presenting options, and me choosing a lesser evil. Bit by bit, choice by choice, he would erode me.

For a moment, I could see myself as he would make me: terrible and fair, brilliant and blinding as a snowstorm, as cold and brutal and beautiful.

I said, "I would rather die for justice than see it ruined."

Your death would achieve nothing. She will have your heart, or a thousand others—and a thousand kingdoms with them.

"No," I said, "she won't."

Kraxikel only smiled his demon's smile. *You will see. In the end.*

16.

Things Remade

When I entered the sitting room of the seven dwarves' private quarters, Red stood from where she'd been crouched by the hearth. Despite her scowl, she looked worried and tired, less witchy than usual, more human.

"Where have you been?"

Washing clothes sounded like a stupid answer, and it wasn't what mattered. "I got lost," I admitted. Lost in my grief. Lost in myself.

She came over to me, still scowling. "Your hands are chapped. You're cold."

She pushed me over to the fire. We sat on a white bearskin and watched the flames. Her shapeless dress made her into a puddle of brown cloth, but she could not hide her beautiful face and brilliant hair and sapphire eyes. Not without magic anyway. She had hidden from me, in the beginning.

"Why did you not want me to know you?"

Her fingers played with the white pelt, twisting the fur. "It was easier."

"It wasn't fair. You knew me." Bitterness edged my voice. I had been exposed; she, hidden.

She frowned. "I think you only let *him* know you."

The broken pieces of my heart grated inside me. The parts of me he had known did not seem very real right now. I could not imagine sighing, smiling, warming against him.

He had seen past my scar more than anyone. It was *I* who had not. It was I who had held myself behind it, behind my coldness, behind my fears.

"Why will you not say his name?" I asked.

"Why do you think?"

"*Red.*"

She looked at me with angry tears brightening her eyes. "Because you love him. And you do not love me."

When she said that, when tears sprang into my own eyes—my first tears in seven years—I understood something: we need no demons to twist us. We twist ourselves, and never even notice. This—*this* was the heart of my pain and fear. This was why I was angry with her.

You do not love me.

That was how I thought she felt about me, and I had not known it until she said it. It is easier to be angry than to say, *You do not love me, and it hurts.* Red had always been braver than I, wiser than I. Of course she understood it first. Of course she said it first.

I had always needed others to reach out first—why could I not conquer that?

The tears spilled down my face. Hers spilled too, and we crawled into each other's arms as we should have done from the beginning. We wept and wept and wept.

For our foolishness and fears.

For our anger and guilt.

For our insecurities and in mourning of all that could not be restored to us—and all we had failed to restore to ourselves.

"I love you," I cried against her.

"I love you," she cried against me.

"I'm sorry you thought that," I said, stroking her hair. It was so much darker than it once had been, darker and deeper than my mother's roses. It was as red as blood.

"I'm sorry," she said, "that I don't know how to be your sister anymore."

She wasn't the Rose of my childhood. She was a seventeen-year-old young woman who had survived things she could not speak of, who had been forced to make decisions she should not have had to make. Those things had changed her. But whatever they had made her into, she was still my sister, and I did not believe that anything could change her heart, not the deepest, most essential parts of it. Even so, I hated that the world had not allowed her to remain sweet and gentle. I hated that I had not been able to protect her from it.

"I'm sorry," I said, "that I wasn't there with you. I'm sorry that you didn't have someone like I did."

I had always known that Halen had saved me. After knowing even the smallest part of what Red had faced, I realized how very lucky I had been.

But Red frowned. "He burned you. I could kill him for that."

There was vengeance in her, as there was in me, as there was in our aunt, but Red had fewer delusions about it. I was not blind to the fact that Kraxikel had approached me, not her. It said something. However frightening and strange and dark Red might be, she was less corruptible than I, her principles less prone to twisting. Either that, or she was too powerful for even the demon king. I preferred the former assumption. I preferred to trust her. It felt *so good* to trust her, to remember how to love her.

I stroked her beautiful red hair. "He is already dead, and he suffered far more than I did. And sometimes ... we hurt the people we love." More tears spilled down my cheeks. I meant her. I meant Halen. I meant Bregas too.

"They tricked you," she said, meaning the dwarves, trying to lift that last fault from me.

Her words gave me no comfort. Even if they were true, there was a bigger truth: I had not known my own heart, and so I had lost it.

Love had been a riddle to me, a lesson I had learned too late, one for which I had paid dearly. I had lost my chance with Halen, had lost it with Bregas. I would not lose my chance again. I would not be a fool again, and so I said once more, "*I love you*, Blood Red."

My sister sighed against me. Touch has power. Silence has power.

Love has power.

Even a broken heart, I now knew, could love—and that meant that even a broken heart had power.

I knew how I wanted to use mine.

I had neglected something in my time under the mountain. I had made a trade. I had given something precious—too precious, and all my thoughts had been on that loss. But I had come here for a reason; I had made that trade for a reason—and that reason still mattered.

I walked the length of the dwarves' feasting hall. This time, I held myself differently. I was serene in my purpose now. I had accepted it; I understood it.

I wore the same traveling frock I had arrived in. I had no more riches with me now than before. But everything feels different and looks different when you bear with you a clear vision of what must be—a clear vision of yourself. I knew what I was. Ambitious and vengeful, yes. Cold, yes. But more.

A witch.

A queen.

A sister.

A lover.

I was many things, and I knew the use I wanted to make of all those pieces. I knew what mattered most, and so I knew exactly what I needed the dwarves to craft.

"She is ready," said one of them.

"She is strong."

"She seeks to know what her pain is worth."

I stopped before their raised table and gazed along the line of seven craggy faces. I could not decide if they were wicked or wise. Strange, how hard it can be to tell the difference. It is a riddle, I guess.

"Tell me, then," I commanded, "what my pain has bought me."

"Wisdom," said one.

"Fortitude," said another.

"A place at our table."

"A place at any table."

"A crown."

"A question."

The last one asked, "And what is your answer?"

"Justice," I replied. "Love."

"Are they the same?" asked the most wizened.

"They must be," I told him, "or they are not truth."

A space opened at the table, a chair appearing that had not been there before. I walked to the edge of the dais and climbed the steps then walked behind the chairs of the dwarf kings and came to my seat. I took it.

I looked out over the company of dwarves, who feasted and drank and laughed. I spotted Red at one of the tables. She looked wary, but I could not tell whether she was wary of me or of the dwarves. Both maybe. She was wise, after all.

My cup brimmed with golden ale, and my plate was mounded with roasted meat and dark, coarse bread. When I picked up my cup, the seven kings lifted theirs.

"To truth."

"To crowns."

"To queens."

We drank, and the ale spilled down my throat to warm my belly. To my right, the oldest and most wizened of the dwarves bit into his hunk of dark bread and watched me from the corner of his eye.

I asked, "What have you done with all you took from me?"

"We have mined from it the truth, shined it to clarity."

"More riddles," I complained.

He grinned, flashing his crooked teeth. "Do not traffic with dwarves if you have not the stomach for riddles."

"But it is truth you truly value."

"A true craftsman works to reveal it. We revealed yours. It is yet to be seen, though, what you will do with it."

I feasted with them, and then we danced. How different it was from Lyric's dances, from the shadowy and grasping spins and turns of her demon court. This was a rough and earthy kingdom, one of shaping and breaking and making. The music clapped out from drums and shrilled from pipes. Dwarves sang and chanted us through the steps.

Heigh-ho! Wheel and blow, clap and spin and dance below!
The mountain rears and plunges low—heigh-ho!
Heigh-ho!

It was a dance of spins and claps and dips, chilling and deep and powerful.

"One more thing we need for our making," said the wizened old dwarf as we bowed to one another under the weight of a thunderous drumbeat.

"What more could I possibly give you?"

Heigh-ho!

"One thing you yet cling to," said another dwarf, taking my hand and spinning me away.

Heigh-ho!

Another clapped beside me. "The thing you hide behind."

Heigh-ho!

"The pain that protects you," claimed another, bowing to me.

Heigh-ho!

"The pain that has made you."

Heigh-ho!

I stopped dead in the middle of the dance. Everyone had stopped, and the music had cut off abruptly. I put a hand to my cheek, suddenly fearing. Much as I hated my scar, it *had* shaped me—and shielded me in a way. It was the thing I retreated behind, that allowed me to feel separate. What would I be without it? What boundary would lie between me and the world?

"You would unmake me."

Dwarvish eyes glittered like onyx. "R*e*make."

A dwarvish voice cracked like a hammer: "Reforge."

Another rumbled: "Unearth."

"Why?" I demanded, not trusting them.

"Because you no longer need to be hidden—but something else does."

A low chant began to whisper through the feasting hall. *Heigh-a-heigh-a-heigh-a-heigh-a-heigh-a.*

"Yield it."

"Give it."

"Let us craft it anew."

The chant rolled out more strongly. *Heigh-a-heigh-a-heigh-a-heigh-a-heigh-a.*

"The strength of the mountain in a silver ring."

"A thing of truth."

"A crown for a queen."

"Its truth unseen."

The chant became a roll of thunder. *Heigh-a-heigh-a-heigh-a-heigh-a-heigh!*

I knelt before the seven kings, my heart pounding, yielding myself to their riddle and their craft. The oldest, wizened and whitened and shriveled by time, took from his belt a small brush, one that might be used to paint or polish.

Heigh-a-heigh-a-heigh-a!

He swept it over the scarred half of my face, from cheek to jaw.

Heigh-a-heigh-a-heigh-a!

At first, I felt nothing because the scarred tissue was hard and dead ... then I felt the tickle of the brush and the loosening of my face.

Heigh-ho!

The dwarf drew back, the brush's tip sparkling oddly. I put a hand to my face, shocked by the tender skin. I put up my other hand to my other cheek. I did not feel whole. I felt exposed and vulnerable.

Heigh-ho!

I felt like something that could be ruined anew.

"Only you would be unhappy," Red observed as we lay down by the fire in the dwarves' sitting room. I would not sleep in their beds again. I preferred to stay out here with Red.

I still could not quite take in the strange smoothness of my face, the way the flesh yielded to expression. I could smile now, a full smile. I didn't smile, however.

"They didn't take it to give me beauty," I said.

"Does it matter why they took it?"

I sat up. My pain had been taken to be reshaped. No—the way I had used my pain had been taken. To hide. To hold back the truth of myself. I had known that, but wearing that realization on my face was troubling me, and I felt strongly the sense of exposure and vulnerability. I felt fear. And I felt like there was some further riddle in this, one I wasn't sure I wanted to solve.

Red sighed. "You haven't even looked at yourself."

"I will," I promised and motioned her to me. She scooted closer and laid her head in my lap. I combed my fingers through her long, beautiful hair until she fell asleep with me watching over her.

A voice came from the shadows. "The swan thought it was a duck."

"I'm too tired for more riddles tonight," I replied, glancing to where the dwarf I had once freed squatted, watching me. The firelight shone against the dark depths of his eyes. He wore neither crown nor cap. His white hair ringed his head in place of either, leaving the crest bald.

He asked, "What use will you make of truth?"

"Are you asking what I will do with the crown?" His amused silence said, *You can interpret it that way if it pleases you.* I still found him insufferable. Well, I could be vague too. "There is more to think about than Lyric. Her demon horde does plenty of evil even without Kraxikel."

"They must be directed," said the dwarf.

"Destroyed," I countered.

"You have no army."

"I will need an ally then."

"What makes the difference between ally and enemy?"

It was one of the earliest riddles he'd posed to me, back in Lyric's dungeon. Thinking from Lyric's perspective, I had answered then that the difference was strength. Now I answered, "Common cause."

"And you seek that ... with the Fae?"

My breath caught. "If you see so much of the future, why not tell me: will it work?"

"It depends on your cause. Fear? Or love?" His dark eyes had never once left my face, and I began to sense that he was here to judge me.

"If you will only answer questions with questions, what is the purpose of my answers?"

"To get to the right question, of course, impatient human queen. I will tell you something, if that is what you want. Fear is a riddle with only one answer. Love is a riddle with more answers than stars in the sky. The knowing of one is not the knowing of all. Love is a work of a thousand points and patterns. See there a bear. See there a cup. See there a chaos of beauty."

I looked down at Red, asleep, her head yet in my lap. I combed my fingers through her silken hair and said, "One star may guide a course."

There was no answer. When I looked for the dwarf again, he was gone.

The next day, I descended into the great cavern at the heart of the mountain, the center of the mining and crafting, the finding and shaping.

Heigh!

Ho!

Fire, burn and glow! Mountain, crack and groan—heigh-ho!

Hammers clapped and bellows pumped and fire danced from the forges. Tongs gripped glowing metal and steam hissed from the barrels. Sparks burst from the anvils and jewels glittered like a rainbow of stars.

I walked among the dwarves, not a ghost of myself this time but something solid and sure. The seven kings worked at a table, laboring along with all the other dwarves, distinguished only by the perfection and fineness, by the heart-piercing beauty of their work. Suddenly, I understood: they were not kings of land and law; the dwarves cared nothing for that. The seven were kings of craft.

The seven together took up a fine gold box from their table. Seven pairs of gnarled and sooty hands bore the box to me, and seven pairs of dark eyes glittered as though with stars, reflecting back the beauty around them.

"It is made."

"It is done."

"It is yours."

I took the box from them. It was heavy. Duty is, I suppose.

"A winter's work."

"A thing for spring."

"A thing of truth."

"A thing for a queen."

Part 4.

A Feast of Magic

17.
Faerie Paths

We emerged from the mountain to find winter melting away. The snow was gone from the branches of the pines and firs, lingering only in the cool, shaded places as patches of fading white. The rest was mud. It wasn't beautiful, but it promised beauty to come. Beside me, Red snugged her cloak around her shoulders.

We had discussed using her cauldron to travel to the cottage, but the cottage wasn't our destination and might not put us any closer to it. We did not have the bear to guide us, but in this I doubted he could help.

As we headed down the slope and toward the trees, trudging through snowmelt and mud, Red did not repeat the questions she'd posed the night before, but I could feel them in the air.

How will we find the border of the Brightwood?

How will we persuade the Fae to open it to us?
I only knew that we must.
I had the crown and, with it, hope. I also had what I'd learned of love and pain and regret. I believed Bregas's father would answer me.

Red had pointed out, with a certain dark humor, that if we could not destroy Lyric's demon horde—and we needed the Fae's help for that—destroying Lyric would only mean falling to the horde moments later. Unless, she had teased, we joined them.

I had not found her funny.

I tried every spell of summoning and seeking and revealing that I knew, to no avail. Red fared no better. We gave up seeking the Brightwood itself and tried seeking the little faeries instead, but none answered.

That night, we built a fire to drive back the chill and the darkness while Red drew out, from her cauldron's magically expansive interior, the provisions the dwarves had gifted us. The bread yet steamed when we broke it open, as though it came fresh from the oven, and the meat was juicy and hot. There was even a skin of ale that never emptied.

"I can try some stronger spells tomorrow," Red offered, passing me the ale.

"Stronger?"

"Darker."

I paused with the ale halfway to my mouth. I had grown so comfortable with Red that I had almost forgotten how dark her magic could be. "You think you could force the Brightwood to reveal itself?"

Red looked away. "Possibly."

"I doubt the Fae would see that as the act of an ally."

"I'm not sure what choice we have."

"There is always a choice," I said quietly.

"And consequences to go with it."

She wasn't wrong, but I wasn't going shatter this moment of peace by dwelling on that. It was a beautiful night. I drank some ale and gazed upward. With the moon a slim crescent, the stars glittered bright through the canopy. My thoughts drifted to Bregas. So many nights I'd sat before a fire with him, lain beside him. All those nights, and I had never managed to tell him that I loved him.

I wondered when my feelings had deepened to love. When he halted at the edge of Red's cauldron to let us escape from Lyric's camp? When he and I had slept before the fire in Red's cottage? Maybe there is no specific moment that love appears; maybe, by the time we notice it, it has long been growing. But I think it took true root in my heart the night Bregas played the flute in the cave, when the faeries danced over his fingers.

"The flute—you still have it, right?"

Red eyed me askance. "Why?"

"Do you remember that night the faeries came to us in the cave?"

"There's no magic in the flute. They came to Bregas, and he was of their kind."

"They came to the music, to what he put of himself in it."

Red dug in the cauldron and pulled out the silver flute. "I guess it can't hurt anything to try, except maybe my ears."

I scowled at her, and her lips quirked as she handed me the flute. This new, sardonic side of her was going to take some getting used to.

I tried out a few notes. I wasn't musical, as Red clearly recalled. Our childhood music tutor had despaired of me. I wasn't so much clumsy as stiff. *Hopelessly practical*, the tutor had lamented. *Too much thinking, not enough feeling.*

But I had learned some things since then. I had learned loss and love. I had learned to reach out, to speak out, to soften. I had learned that not all lessons were for the head; some were for the heart, and it was my heart, broken yet beating, that I played from.

I didn't think about the notes. I couldn't remember a thing about them anyway. Instead, with the stars glittering above me and the fire warming my face, I *felt*.

My love for Bregas and Red.

My love for my parents and kingdom.

Sorrow wove through it all, and yet the love was neither diminished nor darkened by it.

It was, perhaps, the first time in my life that I felt beauty. I had always recognized beauty, been capable of appreciating it, but now I *felt* it. No—I *had* felt this. With Bregas in our most private and truest moments. With Red, when she leaned into me and I into her.

The realization lifted me: that beauty was love and love was beauty. That was why it didn't matter that my face had been ruined and now was not. The pain had mattered; the skin had been irrelevant. Bregas had known that. His understanding of love and beauty had been so much greater mine, but I was learning.

I played all those truths, and more. I played my sorrow for all the harm that Lyric had done: to Bregas, to so many trusting and lonely girls, to the little faeries that were lost and suffering. I played my longing to mend them, to heal that, to make it right.

And they came.

As they emerged from the night to dance, the firelight gilded their lovely wings and painted warmth over their tiny bodies with their clothes of leaves and necklaces of seeds. I rose and played for them, not caring if I looked like a fool whirling around the campfire.

Caught up in the music, I did not think to draw the flute from my lips that I might question them, but the music itself posed the question, and they answered with their dance and with a path of flowers, gently glowing, that led away from our camp and into the night.

As I headed to the path, Red hurried to douse our fire and snatch up her cauldron, then she followed me into the dark woods along the faerie path.

The butterfly faeries were the boldest, but shyer creatures emerged as the night wore on. Twiglike faeries began to scale my cloak until they rode my shoulders and clung to my hair and danced along my arms. Tiny creatures with mushroom caps appeared in my wake, never seeming to move but always behind me on the glowing path.

Red eyed the faeries askance and shooed them away from herself, but they alighted in her hair whenever she wasn't looking. They braided her blood red locks, and when she noticed, she sighed and let them.

Do not go into the woods at night.
Do not follow the faerie lights.
Do not dance and do not sing—set no foot in the faerie ring.

It is strange that sometimes a childhood lesson is the very one we must unlearn.

On through the night I played. Some of the faeries began to sing in sweet, lilting voices, tiny voices, no single one carrying, but they sparkled like dew, a thousand lovely drops that made a pattern. I never took the flute from my lips. I did not want to lose them. I did not want their darkness to return, for it seemed to fade with the music. Most of all, I did not want the beauty to end.

It ended with the dawn.

Not *ended*, perhaps, but one mystery gave way to another—and the new mystery was a towering, arched gate of trees and vines and flowers, tangled into an intricate design. The Brightwood gate made a strange contrast to the doors I had seen under the mountain, where gold and silver and jewels had been fashioned and refined. The Brightwood gate held such a different beauty. Instead of craft, it embodied growth, blending the wildness of nature with fine artistry.

A tangled hedge sprawled out on either side, giving the sense of an immense faerie ring.

The way the gate shimmered, there but not, visible only if I looked at it just right, reminded me of Bregas's antlers. When I could not see them, I could not feel them. I had threaded my fingers through his hair many times, and it had felt as though his antlers did not exist. This was the same. Had I not been dazzled all night by faeries and magic, I might have walked straight through, never seeing the ring, never entering.

As I drew the flute from my lips, ending the song at last, the troupe of faeries shivered with agitation. They chittered and buzzed. My heart ached to see their pain. Once, they had frightened me. Once, I had even struck out at them. I would never do such a thing again. They might not be bound as

Bregas was, but they were shadowed by Lyric's magic, by what she had brought into this world. They suffered.

Some of the coldness returned to my heart at the thought, and my resolve took the place of the now-fading music that had guided me here.

I called out, "Speak with me, King of the Brightwood!"

The gate stood silent and unmoved.

"Leaf and root, bark and branch, vine and bush and bramble—open!"

The hedge shook and rattled in anger, and the little faeries—wing and twig, leaf and flower—shrieked and fled behind me. No magic would force that gate. The Green King would open it or he would not. Bregas had not believed his father would relent, nor had Red, but I knew something that they did not: regret.

All those years of unspoken love and pain and guilt between me and Halen. What might have been if one of us had reached out with a hand or a word? It would not have been easy. Hard things had lain between us. It would have hurt to speak, to be honest with each other. But the memory of silence hurt more.

Bregas's father had been silent with his closed gate. There was regret and pain in that. There was love: wounded and foolish and hurtful.

"You shut out the world, you shut out your kind, you shut out your own son, King of the Brightwood. But it is not too late. I love your son. I think you love him too. I think you would save him. Speak with me, King."

On the gate, vines twined together into a face. Eyes of acorn and berry regarded me dispassionately, and the gate

235

spoke in a voice of earth and otherness, something old and deep. "I care nothing for your troubles of love and war."

"Your son does."

The face of vines showed no emotion. "He is young and foolish."

"And yet, I think, you love him."

"I would see him restored to me."

"And what would you do to see that?"

As the vines untwined and the face faded from the gate, despair crushed me. *No.* Oh, no. I'd been so sure, and without the Fae—

The gate swung inward, revealing a path of blue and white flowers. At my back, the faeries buzzed like a swarm of bees. At my side, Red tensed.

She said, "I did not expect him to let us in so easily."

I felt only relief. "Let us be glad that love is not unique to humans."

When I stepped through, my feet vanishing in clouds of blossom, Red came with me but the troupe of faeries did not. My heart hurt for them as the gate closed with a thump, but I had to move forward to make a way for them later.

Red and I walked along the path. To either side stood trees of every kind, all lovely with spring, many laden with flowers, others bearing tender young leaves, and below them lay a carpet of blossoms and bright grasses. Among the trees stood an occasional white column of stone or a beautiful statue or burbling fountain. Among all that moved the fleeting shapes of the High Fae and other, smaller faeries, ones that had not been caught outside the Brightwood's shelter. I glimpsed sleek cats and bright-feathered birds, and sometimes elegant figures in pale robes. I saw blonde hair and brown and some as dark as earth, though none as dark as mine. Some of the trees seemed to move, but I had no time to study them.

The wood yielded incrementally to stone with more statues and columns and curves of balustrade. Eventually we came upon a courtyard of finely carved pale stone, greenery and gentle flowers adorning every surface. The stone was all so smooth and lovely that I could almost forget how hard it would be at the touch. Nature and perfect artistry, like Bregas. I could not help but love it, even though it was a mystery to me, as he was.

A strange building of stone and woodland stood beyond the courtyard. Though it was tall, I could not say it reared or towered. It was too lovely and fine for such sharp words. It had many faces and many spires but none of the mathematical precision of a human place. More like a tree, it reached and branched in stone and vine. No glass sealed its windows, and birds flew freely in and out.

Red and I crossed the courtyard and mounted stone steps to a set of open doors, where we were met by a beautiful, dark-skinned female with the ears of a cat and a tail that flicked out from behind her, lashing with agitation. Her eyes had slitted, upright pupils.

Without a word, she motioned us in, and we followed her into an antechamber that felt like an extension of the wood. Trees grew through the floor, stone giving way seamlessly to roots and trunks. Light spilled in through windows and doors. At a round doorway—though there was no actual door—our guide stopped us.

"Just you," she said to me.

"My sister—"

"The king would speak only with you."

Red bristled, more catlike even than our guide. "Snow—"

"The box." I held out my hands, one empty, the other returning her flute. Frowning, Red took the flute then dug into her cauldron. She handed me the golden box that held the dwarvish crown.

Without glancing back at Red, I went through the doorway and found myself in what might have been a greenhouse or a library or a beautiful glade. Water spilled from the top of one wall into a little pool, though whether it was a fountain or a waterfall I could not tell. Here, there wasn't much difference.

"You carry trouble into my house, Snow White," said a deep, resonant voice.

I turned but saw only a stone table with an open book and a bent tree beside it. The tree unbent and turned toward me, a face appearing in the wood, the limbs shifting to suggest a body.

"Truth is always troublesome," I replied.

The tree softened into the shape of a man, one dressed in brown and green, bearing a crown of leafy branches. The crown appeared to have grown from his very flesh, and his beard was of leaves. His clothes might have been cloth or leaf, and they moved over his body with seamless ease.

"You speak in riddles," he said.

"Too long with the dwarves, I suppose." My voice came out strained. My eyes were wide upon him, not only for the wonder of him but for the familiarity of his features.

"You see my son in me," he observed. "Or rather, you have seen me in my son."

"How could you have shut him out?" My voice snapped with sudden anger. "You abandoned him."

"He was taken from me."

It was hard to put my anger aside, to not argue with him, but it served nothing. Instead I asked, "And would you not take him back?"

The Green King regarded me for a moment then gestured ahead. We walked past stands that held books, and tables stacked with them. We passed beds of flowers and copses of trees. I was never sure whether my feet were in grass or on stone. Bees hummed and birds twittered. I had never been anywhere more beautiful. If I had a thousand years, I could not tire of this place. And I could not have loved Bregas more than in that moment when I understood the strength of his character and heart that he had chosen to fight instead of hiding here. He had sacrificed himself—to protect what he loved, to do what he thought just.

"Why did you not fight seven years ago?" I asked the Green King.

"Unlike my son, I do not care to meddle in the affairs of men. I want only peace and separateness. Had Bregas not stepped out, she would not have captured him."

"Even if it were in his nature to hide from horror, it would not have lasted. Lyric grows in strength and ambition and madness. She will come for you."

The Green King trailed his fingers along a branch, and flowers bloomed at his touch. "And what do you suggest I do about that, Snow White?"

My own fingers held no such gentle magic, but they tightened on the box that held the crown for which I had paid so dearly. "Help me. Fight her."

"Go to war?"

"Yes." What use in renaming it, in pretending I asked anything less?

"And in exchange for risking my people, what do you offer?"

"Your borders made safe. Your son, returned to you."

"But, Snow White, he is not yours to give."

Before I could explain my plan, a familiar trilling laugh sounded from an archway of stone, and Lyric stepped through, a shimmering vision of silver and auburn and cruelty.

"The king speaks rightly, my dear. The Hunter is not yours to give. He is *mine* to give. Or rather, to trade."

18.

Bad Bargains

Horror filled me. Froze me. For a moment, I could only stare. Lyric's gown flowed like molten silver and her auburn hair hung in smooth, silky waves, but her beauty was terrible, and she looked utterly wrong in the serene garden—especially flanked by stiff, pale-faced demons clothed in shadow. Fresia, perhaps, or not, and one of the others.

This, I had not expected. *Her*, I had not expected, not here. Perhaps I should have. Mad, she might be, but she was a brilliant strategist. How often had she anticipated me in our chess matches?

"What have you done?" I asked hollowly, not sure if I meant Lyric or the Fae King or even myself.

Something slid through the carpet of flowers behind me. I wheeled, ice sparking along my fingertips to frost the golden box in my hands.

Lyric let out her high, sweet laugh. How I hated that sound.

Another slither at my heels had me spinning once more. The Green King had vanished, but the floor of the garden was alive with sliding roots and vines. One curled around my ankle. With a shout, I struck out with a spear of ice. In answer, vines burst up around me, twining and trapping me in a sudden, inescapable hold. In the distance, I heard commotion. Red—!

Winding vines ripped the box from my hands. Shouting, I lashed out with ice, freezing and breaking the branches that thickened and squeezed around me. Thorns slashed my skin.

"Yield!" commanded the King of the Brightwood.

At the sound of Lyric's trilling laugh, I wrenched a hand free of the tangling vines to cast a spear of ice in her direction. I heard her shout of outrage but none of pain, and the king coiled around me like the ivy that strangles a tree. As rage burst from my heart—rage that Lyric could be here, that everything would be ruined before I had a chance to even try—ice raced out along the greenery.

Branches and vines, leaves and berries shaped the king's face, rimed with frost. "Do you think I cannot endure winter—I, the King of the Wood?"

"She would turn the world to ash and rubble."

The Green King replied, "What she does outside the Brightwood is no concern of mine."

"She'll not leave you in peace, whatever she's said."

"She will leave with you—and leave me my son."

"Even if she did, Bregas would not forgive you."

The King of the Brightwood looked away from that, his face of branch and leaf twisting toward Lyric instead. "My son," he demanded.

I could not see Lyric, but I could hear the smile in her voice when she spoke. "I promised your son in exchange for her crown and her heart. You will not get what I promised until I get what *you* promised."

I cried, "Don't trust—"

The Green King hurled me to the ground. I tumbled and rolled through flowers and moss until I came to a stop at Lyric's feet. The box crashed down beside me. Before I could move, my arms and legs were bound in something dark and creeping—shadow.

"Give me my son, Witch-Queen!"

Lyric let out her trilling laugh. She glowed with power, her skin alight, and her silvery eyes danced with madness. As she bent to pick up the golden box, her hands trembled with eagerness, and her pulse fluttered in her elegant, swanlike neck. She gathered the box to her breast, cradling it like a babe.

"I told you," she said breathlessly, "when I have her heart." The king shouted in outrage, but Lyric's attention had shifted to me. "Hello, my sister's child. How you've ripened!"

"What would she think of you?" I seethed. "To see you like this?"

Lyric's fingers stroked my restored cheek. Tendrils of shadows licked out from her fingertips, whispering over my skin. "I do this for her. For *us*. For all women and witches."

"No, you don't. You do it for yourself, as you do all things—and you know it."

243

Fury twisted her face, contorting her beauty into something awful. Then she stood abruptly and shouted to the King of the Brightwood, "We shall feast together, Green King, and then you shall have your son."

When Lyric's demon attendants moved to seize me, I struck out with a blade of ice, slicing straight through the neck of one. Its head toppled, its mouth still smiling stiffly. Lyric flung back her head and laughed. The shadows slithered around me with hungry whispers. I could barely move, but I would fight as hard I could—then I saw Red. Bound in shadows and web, she was being dragged, senseless, through the garden by a spiderlike demon.

"You see your choices, my dear? Fight for yourself—or die quietly for your sister. I don't want to kill darling Rose, not yet. I *so* long for a child. I could have loved one with skin as white as snow and hair as dark as ebony, but … what I truly crave is an heir of my heart. Maybe a year and a day in a cell would soften her to me? I have time to wait, time to watch—now that I have the crown." Lyric hugged the box to herself and called out, "A feast!"

The Green King shaped himself into the semblance of a man. His beautiful face held a deep anger, but his eyes gave away his desperation. Love—selfish and fearful—had led him to open his gate to Lyric, and now he must play her game.

"I will give you a feast, Witch-Queen, and then you will return my son—and we will never see you again."

"Done!" exclaimed Lyric, delight in her voice and madness in her eyes. There were a hundred ways she could twist such a bargain.

More demons appeared as though peeling themselves from the shadows. They latched onto my wrists with their terrible, clawed hands and hauled me to my feet. I stumbled along with them, out of the garden library and into the gentle spring sunlight. The skittering demons made a mockery of the Brightwood's peaceful beauty, of the trees and flowers, the silvery streams and white stones. Birdsong and breeze had been replaced by hissing and chittering.

We traveled along a path of blue flowers, our procession like a parody of the faerie troupe that had led me here. The trees shifted and shivered with agitation, and I caught glimpses of further movement beyond our dark parade, but no help appeared.

We came to a sun-sparkled glade, where a ring of stone tables, with chairs of willow and moss, stood within a ring of trees. I found myself lifted onto the highest table and laid out on my back. Shadows slithered over me, binding me to the table. Red was dragged to another table and forced into a chair, bound and gagged with darkness but conscious now—for all the good it did either of us. Her eyes met mine. They did not plead. She had known too much of horror to hope.

But I hoped.

One small hope.

At Lyric's smiling command, the tables were laid. High Fae in elegant robes, all with the ethereal beauty and wildness that I so loved in Bregas, came to drape the tables with cloth as fine as cobweb. There were ears of foxes and wings of birds. Flowers and vines adorned lustrous hair.

The Fae laid out plates of shell and wood, which held an array of bright greens and earthy mushrooms. Sparkling faerie wine was poured into finely carved wooden cups, and Lyric tasted one after another as though it was her wedding day.

Though the Fae eyed her unhappily, they did as she commanded, as their king had commanded. He appeared here and there, emerging from one tree then another, impatient for things to start and end. But he had made a deal with Lyric, and he was learning that things started and ended as it pleased her, and nothing, nothing, nothing made her uncomfortable. He could glare at her all he liked, but until he fought her, she would only smile and lift one cup of wine after another.

I *begged* them to fight. With my eyes. With the small words, "*Please, please.*" I dared not strike out again with magic, not with Red bound, not with Bregas somewhere unknown. Not without allies.

Then Lyric made her own additions to the feast. Bloody, fist-sized pieces of meat appeared on plates of gold. Not meat, exactly. Her demons hissed and shivered with anticipation. Whether magical or not, the hearts were an abomination, and the Fae drew back in horror. Even the Green King rumbled with displeasure. Lyric only laughed.

As she clapped her hands with delight at the growing feast, I struggled to cling to my hope. Despair was easier. She would kill me. Only when I was dead would she take the crown.

I twisted against my shadowy bindings to see that it lay beside me, torturously close. Noticing my attention, Lyric glided over to me. She seated herself in a chair of woven willow and drummed her elegant fingers on the lid of the golden box. The glow emanating from her could mean only one thing: she had consumed more hearts. Sorsha's, I did not doubt. Others too, perhaps.

Her mad silvery eyes locked on mine. "Did you pay a terrible price, dear one? Did you make a terrible promise?"

"Yes."

Those mad eyes softened with understanding. "Dwarves are twisted little creatures, aren't they? But they are the finest craftsmen in any realm."

"That is mine. Not yours." I was a poor actress. I had not fooled her all those weeks in the castle—my pretense, a waste. Yet in this I could speak truly and deceive her. Though a skilled strategist, she had her blind spots.

"Is conquest so hard for you to understand? You are vanquished, my dear. This is my victory feast. *You* are my victory feast. And I *so* wanted to love you. How different this moment might have been, niece, if you had let me love you. But you refused my love, so I must destroy you instead."

"You know nothing of love."

Lyric dragged a nail down my restored cheek. "You are mistaken. I know too much. I know what it does to people. I know how it turns to pain. I'll not kill you myself, you know. The Hunter will do that. And he will watch me eat your heart." As I shuddered, she leaned down to whisper in my ear. "What do you think that memory will do to him after I've released him? What do you think of the bargain the Fae King has made? I will return his son to him, as promised, but Bregas will be a ruined thing after he's murdered you. I will give him back, but broken."

At her side, shadows gathered into the shape of my love. His face was empty, his antlers rearing high and wreathed in tattered shadows, his light faint among them. His pale sword was in his hand.

From somewhere nearby, the King of the Brightwood shouted, "Bregas!"

But it was the Hunter who stood here, and he yet belonged to Lyric. The price of his freedom was my life. The Green King was willing to see that price paid. Whether Bregas was willing did not matter.

My eyes drifted once more to the golden box.

Lyric said, "I'm almost tempted to place it upon your brow, just for that last moment of your life, but I would rather you see it upon mine. I would rather you know, with your last heartbeat, that everything could have been so different."

With trembling fingers, she opened the box, gasping at the light that sparkled from within. "Oh," she breathed and lifted out a crown of starlight.

Lyric stood from her seat, her eyes dazzled by what had been made from my pain and heartbreak and love. It was beautiful and powerful—and she did not understand it at all.

"Hunter," she commanded breathlessly, "kill her."

"*No.*" Bregas's hand shook on the sword as he raised it. His eyes met mine, and I saw it: a glimmer of him, of his mind, of his heart. He was fighting her with the full force of his enslaved will. The sword turned in his hand, the blade shifting away from me and toward himself.

"*No,*" I echoed. *Wait*, I pleaded with my eyes. *One second. One breath. One heartbeat.*

Wait.

Lyric lowered the crown onto her head, and the stars glittered upon her brow, brilliant and beautiful. Bregas's sword began to plunge—

Lyric screamed. As the truth of the crown blazed into her, she screamed and screamed and screamed. She had wanted a crown that would free her, that would shield her, that would make her impervious to Kraxikel—and she had been all too ready to believe I would choose the same. Like Kraxikel, she had seen my ambition, had known that power appealed to me. But that was not the crown that had been forged from my pain.

My crown was love and justice and truth. When Lyric stole it for herself, what she found was everything she had hidden from, everything she had lied to herself about, all the truths that, deep down, she knew.

Starlight blazed through her, lighting her from within, bursting from her eyes and ears and mouth. She screamed and tears flooded out with the light, the tears of everything she had done, all the pain she had caused, all the evil she could not hide, not in that light.

Bregas gasped and staggered back as the shadows fled from him. My bonds vanished, and I rolled off the table. As Lyric's hold on her demon horde loosened, the shadowy creatures began to shriek. If it had only been those few, we might have overcome them, Bregas and Red and I and the handful of gathered Fae. But as darkness streamed out of Lyric, fleeing the light and the pain of her guilt, that darkness was hundreds of demons. Thousands.

"Snow!" Bregas shouted, but demons spilled between us, a tide of shadow and wickedness.

Claws slashed at me, and I struck out with ice, spearing one demon after another. Bregas's sword flashed and cut, but I caught only glimpses of him among the shadowy throng. Of Red, I saw nothing.

The Fae now fought the battle they should have fought years ago. Vines and branches struck out, spearing and impaling demons everywhere, but too few had gathered here for the feast. Even the Green King was surrounded.

I plunged a blade of ice into the heart of one demon, but the claws of another grabbed me from behind, and I was yanked, shouting, into the air. Claws dug into my shoulders and huge leathery wings whooshed around me as I was borne high above the battle, gaining a clear view of our disaster.

Maybe if I had reached the Brightwood ahead of Lyric, if I had persuaded the Green King before she had, if he had prepared his people and led them, organized, against the horde. Maybe then we could have destroyed the demons. Maybe then the crown might have done its work at an opportune moment. But now…

Shadows swept through the Brightwood, swallowing green, turning beauty to ash. Bregas and a few other Fae warriors spun among the demons, power and grace in their movements, but they were impossibly outnumbered. I spotted Red hurling magic that made the demons hiss and shriek, but she was surrounded. The Green King was a surge of root and branch, but fire burned among his leaves and smoke billowed from him.

Nothing could save us but the crown.

I had no trouble finding it, shining so bright and pure amid the destruction.

The demon's talons dug into me, piercing as I stretched out a finger. As one leathery wing swept down, I brushed it with ice. The creature screamed as its wing froze. We plummeted, spinning, the single working wing trying to slow the fall. The demon's talons released me, but I clung to it to save myself. We crashed to the ground.

Groaning, clumsy with pain, I crawled through blood and ash. Lyric was a husk of herself, shrunken and shriveled as a bitter old woman, her hair sparse and faded, her hands gnarled like ancient roots. The ground was soaked with her tears, and the crown yet glittered upon her brow.

"What have you done?" Lyric wailed. "*What have you done?*"

"Justice."

I tore the crown from her head. She screamed. A ring of blackened flesh marked the crown's judgment. But though what it left behind was ruin, it came away clean, shimmering in my hands.

What use will you make of truth? the dwarf had asked me. I let the cold certainty of what I must do fill my heart as I lowered the crown onto my head. I gasped at the power of its justice and pain and love, and I knew suddenly another layer of this riddle. What did justice and pain and love mean? What did they demand?

As the crown blazed upon my brow, I answered, *Sacrifice.*

A blizzard spun hard and cold in my heart, and I flung out my hands. Snow and ice raged out of me, and the world went white. Wind howled, and the snowstorm ripped through the glade, freezing demon and branch, Fae and witch. I made a winter in spring, and I froze them all to stillness and silence.

It would not be enough. It would hold but a moment, as a snowstorm in spring melts away so quickly. Blood ran down my arms from the demon's talons, and I held out my fingers to let three drops fall into the snow—the red so beautiful against the white.

Bregas stared at me and tried to speak. I was sorry to have taken speech from him, as Lyric had done, but it would be only a moment.

Red stared at me and she, too, tried to speak.

But there is power in silence, and mine said, *I will do this.*

Lyric's tears had frozen into a perfect, smooth circle. A vast mirror, one of regret and sorrow. I summoned it upright. It reflected me, crowned with stars, my face perfect—and utterly irrelevant. It reflected a world of white.

"Mirror, mirror, standing there—"

"No!" The scream came from Red and Bregas, their fear and love overpowering my cold and ice. But it was not enough to stop this.

They would understand in time. They would understand that this was the only way. The least of many evils.

"Kraxikel!" I shouted into the mirror, and the circle went black around the edges, like an ebony frame. I stood before it, the three drops of blood at my feet in the snow, the horror reflected behind me.

The mirror darkened and darkened until it was a window into a place of emptiness.

Then twin lights glowed in the black surface, brightening until Kraxikel's pale face appeared. The demon king smiled, his black lips stretching to display his sharp teeth, his eyes burning like coals.

"*Fairest of the fair, the wicked's heir—you summon a demon king?*"

"I am a queen—you, a king. Bind yourself to me. The fallen witch can be nothing to you now."

Kraxikel's burning eyes went to Lyric's withered form. *"Devious thing you are, Snow White."* He gazed out over the frozen landscape. *"Is this your justice?"*

"Do you like it?"

He smiled. *"Oh, yes."*

"Do you want more of it?"

His long tongue flicked out as though to taste the air. He could not enter this world without me. He needed me to pull him in. His eyes burned with hunger. *"Yes."*

"You will give your demons to me?"

"Yes."

"They are mine?"

"As soon as your hand is mine. Do you give yourself to me, Snow White?"

I stepped toward him, one foot touching the darkness. Kraxikel moved closer, so near to this world and all that I loved. I turned to look out at the mess that revenge and cruelty had made and knew this was the only thing to do, the only hope.

I think the dwarf had known. He had told me the demons must be directed. He had trusted me to understand the riddle in time.

Bregas looked out from the ice, begging me with his beautiful woodland eyes. Red's hand was reaching out. I could not answer either of them—except with this.

I took Kraxikel's hand and said, "I do."

The stars blazed upon my brow, and I felt suddenly in my other hand the hot and horrible leash of that demon horde. They were mine now.

I tightened my grip on them, and I tightened my grip on the demon king—and I stepped back into the mirror.

Kraxikel's face had only a moment to register his surprise before I yanked him and all his horrors into the dark with me.

19.

Light in the Darkness

The demon horde whipped around me like a shrieking gale. The force of my tug had sent them flying into the darkness, a thousand forms whirling into a single, terrifying force that bore me along. The starlight of my crown flickered over rough stone and flashes of pale skin and black claws and hideous wings. Raging along through the maelstrom, always with me, glowed the coal-bright eyes of the demon king that I had tricked.

We seemed to be falling through a tunnel, falling endlessly, until the space suddenly opened. My starlight speared out into the vastness, traveling impossibly far to the distant walls and floor of a rocky cavern. As we fell forever and ever, I thought how it looked like the cavern under the mountain—but empty. Without treasure, without beauty, without craft. A dark, empty, hungry nothingness.

There was no warning. I crashed to the rocky floor like a fallen star, shattering stone into a spider web. I cried out with wordless pain and surrender as the demons burst into shadow and reformed in a hungering, shifting mass around me.

I had no awareness of my hand until Kraxikel yanked his free of it. He threw himself over top of me and hissed furiously into my face, his lips drawing back from his jagged teeth, his eyes burning with rage.

"*Do you have any idea what I will do to you, Snow White?*"

Pain crashed over me like a wave, but it didn't matter. Fear lit inside me—but it didn't matter. I smiled. I had won.

"*You won't be smiling soon, witch.*"

All around us, the demons hissed and skittered in the darkness, hungering. There was only one thing for them to feed upon, here in the nothingness. Kraxikel smiled at the understanding in my eyes. He took it for fear and it was, a little, but it was acceptance too.

"*You have so much magic in your heart, white witch.*"

When the demon king pressed his lips to mine, I tried to draw back, but there was nowhere to go, and I had no strength to do it. My body was a broken and useless thing. Kraxikel inhaled, and the breath was stolen from my lungs.

Kraxikel's long tongue flicked out as he drew back. It chased over his lips as though to capture any stray drop of my magic. That, more than air, was what he had taken from me. My heart shuddered at the loss, at the theft.

He set his lips to mine and inhaled again. And again.

The hungering throng crowded in, sipping from me. Not my lips—Kraxikel claimed the king's place—but from every other bit of me. A thousand greedy demons drank of me, destroyed me, one stolen bit at a time. But it didn't matter.

"I will only tempt another," Kraxikel told me with relish.

But he was wrong. He did not know—even with all that had happened, he did not understand what he and his horde were feasting upon.

They were feasting on justice.

They were feasting on pain and love.

They were eating my sacrifice.

When the demons began to moan, I took no pleasure in it, but I did feel relief. At least it had not been for nothing.

Then the wailing began. And the keening. And the screaming. Their skin began to smoke, awful black tendrils of it rising in the starlight. What they had taken from me was anathema to them; it was poison.

If my body had not been as heavy as stone, I might have shuddered at the sound, at the fury—at the howling of demons all around me.

"What is this magic?" shrieked Kraxikel.

"Love," I told him, or tried to.

He hissed and drew back from me. They all did, shrieking and moaning and skittering into the darkness. Their cries traveled on endlessly through the dark and empty space, a fading echo of destruction, of their undoing.

Eventually, they were gone.

Eventually, I lay alone in the nothingness.

I did not regret, but I did mourn. For Red, who had already lost so much and might not forgive me. For Bregas, who had suffered and loved and from whom I had withheld the truth of my own feelings. For myself, because I had not had a chance to correct that mistake. For myself, because I accepted this, but I was still frightened and cold and so very alone.

The light of my crown faded and faded and faded—until it was gone.

When a new light bloomed in the darkness, I thought, *It is nice, that death should be bright and beautiful.*
With it came a whispering chant.
Heigh. Ho.
Queen lost below.
Light, dim and blown—heigh-ho.
Heigh. Ho.
Queen, your darkness flown.
Love will claim its own—heigh-ho.
Even now ... riddles. I might have laughed, but I could only watch as the light grew, floating through the vast space, bright at its center but diffusing endlessly into the nothingness. No—it did shine on something.

The white light—a witch light—brought out a smooth young face from the darkness. Was death so kind as to give me that final image? Oh, Red. So fine and fierce. So strong and strange.

"I love you," I breathed.

The image bloomed into a whole vision of her, brownish-red cloak and all, even the scowling sapphire eyes under the slashing red brows. Her hand reached out to touch my cheek.

"I love you too, sister." Even so, she was angry with me. I had hidden this last thing from her, after all.

I said, "I'm sorry that I hurt you."

She answered, "I forgive you."

Her words soothed me as nothing else could have done. They were not a denial of my words but a recognition of them. Acceptance.

When something moved out from behind her, shuffling through the dark, I whimpered. The demons had returned— they would take this vision from me.

"Peace, sister," whispered my blood red Rose, and seven craggy faces surrounded me. Seven crowns adorned seven heads, and seven fingertips touched my brow.

I said, "I solved the last riddle, friends."

"You did," said one.

"But not," said another.

"There is no last riddle."

"Here is another."

"What gift can be accepted and returned at the same time?"

My eyes went to Red. "Love."

"Love," one king echoed.

"Love," another echoed him.

A tear slid from my eye. "I don't want to die in this place."

Red's jaw hardened, and she looked to the dwarves. The oldest and most wizened shook his head. "She has but moments left."

A tear slid from my other eye. "I wish I had told him that I love him."

Red's fingers stroked my hair. "He knows, sister."

I could not help that disappointment pressed down upon me. I had wanted to say it. Words have power, and I had wanted to give him mine. It is a hard final lesson that we do not always get to correct our mistakes.

Red's eyes avoided mine, and I sensed something troubling her. I wanted nothing more left unsaid. If I had but moments left, I would use them well. I asked, "What is it?"

"I was selfish," Red admitted, sapphire eyes meeting mine. "I thought only of myself and my love. I did not think of yours, beyond me. I did not think of his. As soon as you vanished into the mirror, I leaped into the cauldron. I had ... I had already prepared the spell, you see. To return to the mountain."

She amazed me. "You knew."

"I knew *you*, sister, and so I suspected. I had already found the path here—with some help." Her eyes flicked to the dwarf that I had freed from Lyric's dungeon. If I'd had the strength, I would have scowled at him for leading her to such a place. Red teased, "What did you think I was doing all those months?"

My eyes returned to her. "Clever Red."

"Sneaky," she countered. "But I left him. The last thing I saw was his keening. I am sorry, sister. I thought only of myself."

"And of me," I reminded her.

"And of you."

"I forgive you," I said, as she had to me, but something troubled me, a fear. "Do you understand, my red sister, that my love for you is not lessened by my love for him?"

A tear slid from her eye, and I knew that this had troubled her. She said, "The dwarves gave me a riddle when I came to them."

"Of course they did." I was too weak for my voice to carry my amusement, but I felt it. It was a good thing to feel.

Red posed their question: "What thing, when divided, grows?"

I had some little strength left, and I used it to smile. "Love."

"Love," she agreed. She tried to return my smile but did not manage it. For her, the answer to this riddle was coming too late. She would bear the lesson with regret. I ached for her, but I could not change that.

One of the dwarves said, "There is yet a little power in the crown."

"We could remake it."

"Craft it again."

"To hold the queen."

"To hold her words."

"To hold a moment."

"To hold death."

Hope flickered in my heart like a tiny flame. "Please," I whispered. Then to Red I said again, "I love you." They are words that you cannot say too many times.

Tears slid down her cheeks and dripped onto my face to blend with mine. "I love you too, my white sister."

She drew back as the dwarves plucked the remains of the crown from my brow. Each taking a seventh part of it, they surrounded me. For once, they worked without sound, silent in their crafting.

My body was beyond pain, beyond feeling, but I sensed a closing in, under and around me. Above, Red's witch light gleamed across a translucent panel that the dwarves lowered and lowered until I was closed in a case of glass.

I could still hear and I could still see. I wished I could have thanked them for not shutting me into the dark.

The dwarves lifted the glass case and me with it. As Red walked ahead with her witch light, the dwarves bore me along on their shoulders. We moved through darkness for a long, long time. Then Red's light caught rough stone and the glitter of hidden gems and thin veins of silver and gold.

In the distance, I heard the clinking of hammers and the swaying of song.

We emerged from a tunnel into a cavern—the great cavern of the dwarves' crafting, where a hundred fires of making burned. As we passed, the hammers ceased and the bellows stopped and the song turned to silence. The dwarves dropped to their knees and bowed their heads.

Red and the seven kings bore me up the slope and out of the cavern, and we traveled the long passageway, past the doors of silver and gold. We emerged into sunlight.

Tears slipped from my eyes, tears of gratitude and relief. Red had given me the sun and the sky and the world.

In the distance, a stag bellowed, the sound long and loud and mournful. I had no strength left to summon him, but Red summoned him for me.

At the base of the mountain, the dwarves lowered me into the wildflowers and grasses. The snow and mud were gone. Summer had come.

The stag bellowed, agonized, from somewhere nearby. I ached for him, for his loss, but I had learned that a heart has room for loss and love together.

When Bregas dropped to his knees beside the glass case, his face was pain, and his antlers shimmered in and out of sight like he could scarce control his form. He moved to tear away the lid, but Red stopped him, warning, "She will have only a moment. Use it well."

Bregas closed his eyes, calming himself. His rack of antlers solidified, and when he opened his hazel eyes, their woodland depths held all his love—and acceptance. I was glad. I wanted him in this last moment, not his fear and pain. His hand was steady as he lifted the lid of the glass case.

"I love you," I said at once, tears streaming from my eyes. "*I love you.*"

He leaned down to me, beautiful and strange, his magnificent rack of antlers free of shadows, his light pure and mysterious. As his lips pressed into mine, he said, "And I love you."

Light and warmth filled me, flooded me until, for a moment, there was no space in me for anything else. There was only Bregas and our love.

When he lifted me from the glass case, I smiled. I would rather die in his arms than in there. His arms wrapped around me, and I felt the embrace, where I had felt nothing before. I felt his strength and warmth. Then I felt my own arms lift and close around him. It was a beautiful, beautiful dream.

But … it was no dream. I felt my heart beating in my chest. And I felt my legs in the grass. And I felt his warm, strong body against mine.

I breathed in, tasting the clean air and the traces of his woodland scent. I drew back, looking at him in shock and a little fear. A streak of white now threaded through his hair from his temple. "Oh, my love, what have you done?"

One of the dwarves said, "He has given love."

"He has given life."

"He has shared his grace."

"Bregas—"

"I love you," he said.

I ached that he would give such a thing to me. I almost said, *I am not worthy of that.* But it was his to give, to choose, and so I smiled at his love. I had said my words, and touch has power too, and so I kissed him instead.

20.

Growing Things

I found Red in the garden. I still couldn't quite look at the apple tree. At first, I had thought to cut it down, but if I were to destroy everything Lyric had touched here at the castle, there would be nothing left. I had to believe that wounds could heal, that new memories could bring love where there had been loss.

Red was sitting by the fountain, her fingers trailing through the water. She looked uncomfortable in her wedding finery. Green silk and blue ribbon adorned her, and diamond pins held up her heavy locks of red hair.

Her lips quirked as I approached. "You bring sweets to entice me? I'm not a wild animal."

"I bring them because you like them." I seated myself on the edge of the fountain and set the plate of honey cakes between us. "And because you left the feast before dessert."

Red sniffed. "Too many people."

"Royal weddings tend to be crowded," I replied wryly.

"Royal castles too."

"Hm."

Red picked up one of the honey cakes and bit into it, her expression softening at the flood of sweetness. Her eyes traveled across the garden to the castle walls. "I like it better now."

"A mouthful of honey always improved your mood."

She rolled her eyes, and I smiled. I knew what she meant. Vines now grew up the many faces of the castle, twining around the windows, draping the statues, and curling along the crenellations. Flowers bloomed everywhere, little bursts of white and pink and blue. I preferred their tender beauty to jewels. And I preferred my crown of leaves and berries and flowers to any ring of silver or gold that I might have worn.

Red watched my crown for a moment—because it wasn't just greenery. The little faeries had made themselves a part of my decoration and would not leave me alone. They had fluttered their wings atop my head all through the ceremony and the feast, annoying Bregas mightily by cheering every time he kissed me.

Red sighed, and I felt the rest of her statement coming. "I like it better, but I still ..." She trailed off. She didn't want to hurt me.

"Won't stay," I finished for her. "I know."

She brushed at the crumbs of honey cake that littered her dress.

"I love you as you are, Blood Red."

She sniffed and looked away. I wasn't hurt. It wasn't about me. She was her own person, and I didn't expect her to change for me or live for me. I held out my hand, and she took it. Her fingers were slightly sticky.

"I'll stay a few more days," she promised.

"Thank you," I said and leaned into her and kissed her cheek.

She squeezed my hand then released it to reach for another honey cake. "Bregas is waiting for you."

As I walked along the path to the castle, the roses bloomed around me. I smiled, touched by her gesture. There are so many ways to say, *I love you.*

I found Bregas in the room we had taken as our own, one high in the castle. The roof was gone, the room open to the sky. A tree grew in the middle, and our bed was of moss. Birds flew in and out, and faeries darted this way and that, hanging garlands laden with berries and acorns.

The beauty was a wedding gift from the Green King. It would take Bregas time to forgive his father, but at least a hand had been reached out. It was a beginning.

Bregas looked more frazzled that I had ever seen him. I laughed as three faeries started braiding his hair while he wasn't looking. He wasn't looking at *them* because he was looking at *me.*

He strode across the room toward me, his sudden movement dislodging the faeries and sending them tumbling. When he bent to kiss me, a chorus of tiny cheers rang out around the room.

"Go away!" he scolded them.

I gave him a disapproving look. "Be kind."

"This is our day," he huffed.

"Love shared, grows."

"But some things are private."

I smiled. "True." I called all the little faeries to me, every wing and leaf and twig. "Thank you, my friends. Now will you *please* let me have him to myself for a while?"

My face was peppered with kisses and Bregas was surrounded by a frenzy of faeries, then they all darted away to leave us alone. I reached up and teased the new braids from his hair, fingering the white lock. He had chosen me, shared his grace with me, diminishing his own life and magic to restore mine. And to that gift he had added his presence here.

His father had made the castle bloom, but it was still a castle. It wasn't the Brightwood, and he had been a prisoner here. Sometimes memories darkened his eyes as we walked along one hallway or another.

"Will you be happy here?" I couldn't help asking it. I wanted him with me, but I didn't want him unhappy.

"We will make this a good place," he said.

"One of justice."

"And love," he added, taking me into his arms and joining his lips to mine.

About the Author

Katherine Buel is a fantasy novelist and avid horsewoman. She has an MFA from Northern Michigan University and has lived in eight different states.

Printed in Great Britain
by Amazon